MIKE HAMEL's MATTERHORN the BRAVE

No. 3

Pyramid Scheme

MIKE HAMEL's MATTERHORN the BRAVE

No. 3

Pyramid Scheme

LIVING INK BOOKS

Writing Worth Reading

Pyramid Scheme
Copyright © 2007 by Mike Hamel
Published by Living Ink Books, an imprint of AMG Publishers
6815 Shallowford Rd.
Chattanooga, Tennessee 37421

ISBN: 978-089957835-4

First printing—July 2007

Cover designed by Daryle Beam, Bright Boy Inc., Chattanooga,
    Tennessee
Interior design and typesetting by Reider Publishing Services,
    West Hollywood, California
Edited and proofread by Pat Matuszak, Sharon Neal, Dan Penwell,
    and Rick Steele

Published in association with the literary agency of Sanford Commu-
nications, Inc., 16778 S. E. Cohiba Ct., Damascus, OR 97089

Printed in Canada
13 12 11 10 09 08 07 –T– 8 7 6 5 4 3 2 1

Library of Congress Cataloging-in-Publication Data

Hamel, Mike.
    Pyramid scheme / by Mike Hamel.
        p. cm. -- (Matterhorn the brave series ; v. 3)
    Summary: Transported to ancient Egypt by a mysterious stranger, Matterhorn
and his friends soon find themselves involved in a dangerous search for the
heretics who have begun a secret conquest of the Earth.
    ISBN-13: 978-0-89957-835-4 (pbk. : alk. paper)
    [1. Space and time--Fiction. 2. Egypt--History--To 332 B.C.--Fiction. 3.
Christian life--Fiction. 4. Science fiction.] I. Title.
    PZ7.H176Pyr 2007
    [Fic]--dc22
                                                        2007014672

The characters and stories in
this series exist because of Susan,
who made them all possible.

Contents

Prologue

MATTERHORN didn't have time to protect his face from being smashed into the stone. But instead of hard rock, he felt a tightening slick surface as if he were being shrink-wrapped in plastic.

He could not move.

He could not breathe.

He was trapped between moments, suspended in time.

Is this what it feels like to be dead, he wondered? A light show danced across the outside of his clear envelope. There was no sense of motion inside. Then everything faded to deep black and he heard rustling. A wave of heat dried the sweat on his face. The darkness became a shade lighter.

"Where are we?" Jewel asked in a shaky voice.

Good, Matterhorn thought. He wasn't alone. And he probably wasn't dead. Before he could say anything, he heard the Baron reply, "I don't know. Wherever it is, let's hope the wraiths can't follow us. Matterhorn, are you okay?"

"I think so. Where's Nate?"

The question rang in the void like an unanswered phone.

As Matterhorn's eyes adjusted, he made out two shapes. There should have been three. Had Nate missed the magic exit? Had the wraiths grabbed him?

"What happened?" Jewel wanted to know. "Who was that stranger?"

"My name is Elok," came an unexpected response.

A shrouded shape glided in front of the Travelers. The man's smooth head and bull neck reminded Matterhorn of a brass bullet.

His movement raised a cloud of dust. Jewel coughed and said, "I have a feeling we're not in Kansas anymore."

Elok smiled. "Not even close."

Matterhorn was in no mood for guessing games. The harrowing events of the last week had made an omelet of his emotions. He had barely escaped drowning in a flooding volcano only to be captured by wraiths and forced to march for a day. His broken arm hurt like crazy. His nerves were shot. He had just been shoved through a rock wall. "Where are we?" he demanded, raising his Sword. "Is this First Realm?"

"If it were," Elok replied, "you would be dead and that would be lost." He pointed at Matterhorn's Talis.

"How do you know that?" the Baron challenged as he stepped forward, switchwhip in hand.

"There is no cause for alarm," Elok said. His gaze moved from the Sword to the whip, while his body remained relaxed. "I serve the Maker and the royals of the Realm. As to your present location, you are still on Earth. In Egypt to be precise."

Matterhorn let out a sigh and lowered the weapon. It remained lit and formed a halo around them.

"Thank you for saving us," Jewel said. She reached her right hand toward him in a Traveler's salute while concealing something in her left hand.

Elok leaned away and warned, "Do not be so quick to use the Band of Justice, especially on one who has given no cause for mistrust."

Jewel blushed at the exposure of her secret intent.

"Talis are not to be used lightly," Elok said. "Put the Band away and use your common sense. What does it tell you?"

Jewel did so and stared up into Elok's unblinking gray eyes. "You saved our lives," she sighed after a bit. "I suppose that's enough for now."

The Baron put away his switchwhip and shed his pack. "If you used a portal, then we're either in the Great Pyramid at Giza or in the Valley of the Kings. What time period?"

"We are in the Valley," Elok said. "1325 BC, local time."

"What are we doing here?"

"Please sit," Elok motioned to a pile of dusty furniture. "I will explain."

"Not until I know what happened to Nate," Matterhorn said, splashing Sword-light this way and that. They were in a vaulted storeroom with what appeared to be life-size comics on the walls. Odd pieces of furniture and household items were piled everywhere, including clay pots full of decaying foodstuffs and reed hampers crammed with clothes.

"Calm down," Elok said. "Your companion has been watching from the shadows to see what I will do. Is that not so, Nate?"

"Maybe." Nate followed his voice into the light— and tripped on a carpet.

Elok caught the stumbling bushman. "Your caution is wise," he said.

Nate regained his feet and smiled. "Didn't have a chance to look before we leaped. Why Egypt?"

"My master and I are here on the business of the Realm," Elok said. "Business for which the Band of Justice would be of great help. Because we knew where it had been hidden I went to retrieve it."

"How did you know to show up when you did?" Matterhorn asked.

Elok ran a hand over his smooth scalp and admitted, "The timing was a divine coincidence. I did not foresee your arrival at the portal, or your need of rescue."

Matterhorn pondered this as he sat down against an elaborately carved trunk. The Talis were safe; that was the important thing for now.

But what was he doing in Egypt?

And how would he get home?

Q and A

MATTERHORN hadn't slept in two days. His good arm felt as limp as his broken one. His legs were sprawled out in front of him as lifeless as speed bumps. The only part of him not going offline due to exhaustion was his curiosity. But before he could ask the mysterious Elok another question, Nate spoke up.

"Bonzer trick back in the cave, mate."

"Was it a projected image?" the Baron guessed. "A hologram?" He dusted off an ornate wooden chair and straddled it backward, arms folded over a gilded lion's head.

"Close," Elok said with the hint of a smile. Before finding a chair of his own, he took something from his pocket and lit the torch in a nearby wall niche.

Jewel curled up on a small cushion while Nate perched atop the chest against which Matterhorn had collapsed. "Go on," he said.

"When I arrived at the portal," Elok said. "I saw two Bigfoot dragging you forward. After the true Sasquatch tried to rescue you, I realized your captors were wraiths. It was not hard to guess what they wanted; though I doubt they expected to find so many Talis in one place." His gaze swept the tired faces before him.

"Knowing you were headed to certain death," he continued, "I created a diversion and brought you here with the aid of a time-sheet."

"What's a time-sheet?" Jewel asked.

"I've used the portals a fair bit," the Baron said, "but I've never experienced anything like the trip here. It felt like being vacuum-packed in a baggie."

Elok straightened his back and pulled a folded square of clear material from beneath his cloak. "A time-sheet unfolds to allow portal-to-portal travel without going through the Propylon."

"I didn't know that was possible," the Baron said, "except with this." He took out the multisided Traveler's Cube that could open a portal anywhere in time-space.

"There is nothing like the Traveler's Cube," Elok said. "A time-sheet only functions from one portal to another."

"How does it work?"

"It encases those who step through it and shrinks to the size of a photon." Elok spread his arms wide and then brought his hands together and squeezed them. "The properties of the photon are instantly passed through the zero-point energy field via nonlocal resonance to a photon in the desired portal. Then the time-sheet materializes, expands, and unfolds."

"That's clear as mud," Jewel muttered.

The Baron frowned. "Why haven't I heard of time-sheets before?"

"Because only a select few Praetorians have them," Elok replied. "They are a closely held secret."

Sucking in his breath, Matterhorn asked, "Are you a Praetorian?"

Elok patted his bald head comically. "Do I look like one of the elite Guardians of the Propylon? I am a servant. And my master will be most anxious to meet you. I cannot take you to him tonight, dressed as you are. I will return in the morning with food, drink, and clothes. You will be safe here; this tomb is sealed. Can I do anything to make you more comfortable before I go?"

"Yeah," Matterhorn joked, "you can fix my broken arm." He lifted his yellow sling and winced. The injury had resulted from an earthquake a few days previous.

Elok knelt in front of Matterhorn and partially unfolded his time-sheet. He rested one palm on the transparent material as it floated in midair and carefully arranged his fingers much the same way Matterhorn had seen the Baron adjust the Traveler's Cube. When satisfied, he said to Matterhorn, "Your arm, please."

Matterhorn leaned forward cautiously and unslung his left arm. Elok took hold behind the elbow and slowly pushed it into the clear membrane. Matterhorn watched his flesh disappear inch by inch. He could still feel his missing member; it tingled and itched, but there was nothing to scratch!

In a few moments, Elok drew the arm back healed and whole.

Matterhorn wiggled his fingers and made a fist. "A-amazing," he stuttered as he rubbed the bones. There was no trace of the break, not even a dent.

"How'd you do that?" Jewel cried.

"I did nothing," Elok said, getting to his feet. "Matterhorn's body repaired itself. It just needed some time. About two months to be exact."

"Pushed his arm into the future," Nate said.

Elok folded away the time-sheet. "You have heard the saying, 'time heals all wounds.' That is not always true, but in this case it is."

"Thank you," Matterhorn said, standing to give Elok a Traveler's salute with his good-as-new arm.

Returning the gesture, Elok said, "You are welcome." He saluted the others in the same fashion. He stopped at the Baron and touched his ear. "I see you have U-Trans. Good. Give them to me and I will set them for the current dialect."

Only then did Matterhorn notice the clear plug in Elok's own ear.

"Great," the Baron said. He removed the universal translator's earplug and throat patch and placed them in their carrying case. Matterhorn, Nate, and Jewel did likewise.

Elok walked to the doorway and paused. "One more thing. Do not leave this room. The tomb has been booby-trapped to discourage grave robbers." He rubbed his chin and said, "Discourage is not accurate. I believe the correct term is dismember."

Spider Man

HE'S right about this place," Nate said after Elok left. "The pharaohs' tombs are half museum, half bank, and half torture chamber. Security measures are lethal." His sly grin showed his faulty math was calculated to make a point.

"I don't suppose they included a ladies' room in their grand design," Jewel complained.

"The dead don't hear the call of nature," Nate said.

"Well, nature still has my number. If you gentlemen will excuse me." Jewel put on the silver-lined cap the Baron had given her. Its headlamp began to glow softly as she moved toward the dark hallway.

"Didn't you hear Elok?" the Baron said.

"I'll be careful." She adjusted her cap downward to pick up Elok's footprints on the dirty floor. "All I have to do is follow these and I'll be fine."

The Baron started to get up. "Maybe I should go along."

"Not necessary."

"It's dangerous."

"I can take care of myself."

"Sure you can; that's not the point."

"I won't go far."

"I still think—"

"You two sound like brother and sister," Matterhorn cut in. "Just let her go." He had grown to respect Jewel in the short time they'd been together. She was tougher than most guys he knew while being prettier than most ladies.

"Really," the Baron said. "I've never had a sister."

"And I don't have a brother," Jewel echoed. "Is this nagging what I'm missing?" There was a giggle in her tone. She stuck out her tongue at the Baron and left the room.

Since he was up, the Baron came over to check out Matterhorn's miraculous healing. He tickled Matterhorn's wrist and said, "Our bodies are aged to adulthood when we travel. I just didn't know the effect could be localized."

"Does this mean my arm is older than the rest of me?" Matterhorn asked.

"I suppose so," the Baron replied. "But I wouldn't worry about it."

Matterhorn loved becoming instantly older when time-traveling. He loved being able to do things he couldn't do as a twelve-year-old. From out of nowhere a dark question slid across his mind like a storm cloud. Did this wonderful privilege come with a price? He looked at the Baron, who was thirteen years old at home, and asked nervously, "Are there any negative effects from the growth spurts we experience?"

Aaron let go of Matterhorn's arm and shrugged. "I told you before, traveling is hard on the body. Matter is dissolved into energy and its pattern is instantly reconstructed at its destination. The molecular bond is weakened with every trip. It eventually becomes so feeble that the body can't be reassembled. That's why Travelers retire in their twenties, if not before."

Matterhorn thought of the science fiction movies where people were dematerialized and beamed across space. Evidently, if a Traveler took one too many trips, it would be a one-way journey.

"From what I understand," the Baron continued, "it's even riskier for First Realmers to time-travel. Every trip is like playing Russian roulette. That's why even the Praetorians travel only with the protection of a Talis."

"Let's find some bedding," Nate spoke up.

Matterhorn lit his Sword and went to check the far corners of the room. He saw a few animal skins and some thick rugs rolled up like giant sausages. With the tip of the Sword, he sliced the binding on a carpet and began rolling it out with his foot.

Suddenly a blur of brown raced up his pant leg, sending a bolt of terror down his spine. He slapped furiously at the bulge, which got halfway up his thigh before suffering a direct hit. Matterhorn did a one-legged jig until the dead arachnid slid down a trail of its own blood and plopped onto the carpet.

Nate and the Baron ran over with the torch, only to find Matterhorn jumping up and down on a squishy red spot.

"Biggest spider I've . . ." Matterhorn rasped between gulps of air. "Up my leg . . . almost got . . ."

Nate examined the pulpy stain.

"What kind?" Matterhorn wanted to know.

"Hard telling from what's left. Tarantula maybe. Or wolf spider. Maybe a field mouse."

"It was a spider!" Matterhorn insisted.

"Better check for bites then."

Matterhorn handed the Sword to the Baron. He dropped his pants and began searching for tiny teeth marks on his red-streaked skin. How was he supposed to tell the difference between his blood and the spider's? Normally he liked spiders; he just didn't like big ones crawling on his person. Satisfied he was unhurt, he hitched up his trousers and said, "I'll hold the light; you check for more vermin."

Very carefully, they selected their bedding and soon had a sleeping circle spread around a low couch, which they reserved for Jewel. What was taking her so long, anyway?

Not wanting to go to sleep until she returned, they occupied themselves with the vivid scenes and weird symbols on the walls and rounded ceiling.

"Can you read any of this?" the Baron asked.

"Some," Nate replied as he traced a character with his fingertip. "Read a few texts on hieroglyphics in the library at Alexandria. This scene's from the *Book of Gates*."

"The Egyptians sure had a lot of gods," Matterhorn said as he scanned the colorful images of people bowing to everything from serpents to the sun.

"There is only one *Maker*," the Baron said. "Everything else is *made*. The Egyptians don't realize that, so they worship creatures rather than the Creator. If only they—"

A wild shriek from deep inside the pyramid cut off the theology lesson and sent the Travelers scrambling for the doorway.

Cat Call

JEWEL had carefully followed Elok's footsteps past the life-size granite guards on either side of the storeroom doorway. In the faint glow of her headlamp, she made out only a few prints at a time. Curiosity pulled her farther than she needed to go and, in a short while, she reached an intersection. Elok's trail went straight across the center of the crossway. But as she moved through the junction, Jewel heard a small sound to her right.

The noise stopped her feet and her heart at the same instant. There was something *alive* in this shrine of the dead! That should have sent her scrambling back to the safety of the storeroom. Instead, she turned right and headed down the hallway toward what sounded like a *meow*.

Blood pounding in her throat and ears, she inched past a sealed burial chamber with its stone sarcophagus and treasure-filled anteroom. Keeping her left hand on the wall and her right hand in front of her, she stiff-armed her fear and crept forward.

A second meow, longer and more forlorn than the first.

What was a cat doing in here? Jewel wondered. Did Egyptians take their pets to the grave? If so, how could an animal survive in a sealed tomb?

She hated dark enclosed spaces. But unlike many people with phobias, she knew exactly where her sense of intense dread came from. She could pinpoint it to the day. She had been five years old and inquisitive as a monkey about everything. On that particular afternoon she had crawled headfirst into a narrow cave and had gotten stuck.

It had been hours before her father had found and freed her. Dark and terrible hours full of shallow dirty breaths, and painful cramps. The trauma left a deep scar on her psyche that the blackness around her clawed open.

To make matters worse, the figures on the wall seemed to be watching her. Once, when she spun around, she caught a pair of red eyes winking in the passing light. She tried to whistle but her mouth had gone dry. She didn't have enough saliva to lick a stamp.

The eerie silence was more frightening than the soundtrack of any horror movie. And when a wisp of spider web brushed her face, Jewel bit her lower lip to keep from screaming. Bad enough to be afraid of the dark, she didn't want the guys to think she was a—well, a girl! The Baron would never let her out of his sight again. She was a Chinook and able to take care of herself, thank you very much!

Another meow somewhere ahead strengthened her resolve. She quickened her pace. Why couldn't her lamp be brighter? Her thick hair must be blocking some of her body heat that should be powering the light. Only her fierce love of animals kept her inching past narrow doorways slit into the corridor like bloodless cuts. In between these gashes stretched gruesome scenes of Egyptian armies slaughtering their enemies in Technicolor gore. Carbon black prisoners in gypsum white kilts marched across the ochre walls to their doom.

Jewel lowered her gaze in disgust and watched the dust swirling in small clouds around her ankles.

After another right turn, the passage widened into a vaulted gallery with even more graphic artwork. Not far down this new hallway Jewel stumbled over a protruding stone. She caught her balance and never realized that the floor behind her was sinking into the depths, leaving a twenty-foot chasm in her wake.

She had triggered what the designers of this pitfall called the Winepress. Any weight landing on the now sunken floor would release the sidewalls. Tons of sand behind each would force them together and flatten anything in between to the thickness of grape juice.

But Jewel knew none of this as she pushed on to the next intersection, where she paused to take in a magnificent mural. The beautifully detailed scene from the *Book of the Dead* showed the weighing of the heart ceremony in which Anubis decided the fate of the deceased.

She stooped to study a kneeling figure in the bottom panel. That's when she saw them: two blue orbs glowing near the floor on the other side of the junction. The eyes were different from the red ones that had been spying on her. Her feeble headlight couldn't catch the rest of the animal before it skittered through a doorway, but she could sense the feline's fear.

Without thinking, Jewel darted through the intersection.

A low rumble rolled into her wake. She turned as a huge slab of the wall slid across the passage. Had she jumped immediately, she might have made it back—but that would have meant abandoning the cat.

Instead, she screamed louder and longer than ever before in her life.

The stone partition slammed shut, chopping the shriek in two.

Obstacle Course

THE desperate cry brought Nate into the hall faster than lightning. Matterhorn and the Baron followed like thunder. "Let me go first," Matterhorn insisted, the blade in his hand becoming more brilliant as he spoke. He led them to the place where Elok's footprints went straight while a smaller set broke off at a 90-degree angle. Veering right, they chased the solo prints down corridors of funerary splendor to where the floor suddenly disappeared.

If not for Matterhorn's Sword, and the goalie drills in his other life that had given him the ability to stop and change directions on a dime, he might have fallen to his death.

The light reached across the yawning chasm but could not penetrate to the bottom of its blackness. "Jewel!" the Baron cried. "Are you down there?" His ears strained to go where his eyes could not, but it was useless. The pit stayed as silent as a grave. "There's no way she made it across that hole," he finally managed.

"But she did," Nate said calmly, pointing to the other side of the pit.

Matterhorn lifted the Sword as high as possible. He could just make out the footprints continuing down the hall.

"Jewel must have hit a tripwire or something," the Baron guessed. "This trap wasn't meant to keep trespassers out, but to keep them in—forever."

"So, how do we get across?" Matterhorn asked.

Nate motioned them back the way they had come. Then, without warning, he turned and raced toward the gap like a ferret on rollerblades. He launched himself from the edge and landed on the other side, somersaulting twice and coming to his feet with graceful ease. Wiping the dirt from his backside, he called out, "Like jumpin' a billabong. Who's next?"

"We don't have the same springs you do," the Baron said. "Don't you know that white men can't jump? What if we don't make it?"

"What if we don't even want to try," Matterhorn muttered.

"Get the rope from your pack," Nate said. "Use it as a safety line."

Because Matterhorn had the light, he ran back for the rope. A short time later, he had one end of the yellow nylon cord around his waist while Nate held the other. Still, Matterhorn hesitated. Although his arm was healed, the memory of snapping bone remained painfully fresh. He didn't want an encore. Why not stay here and let Nate and the Baron go after Jewel?

He gave himself the by-now-familiar lecture: Because he had promised Queen Bea he would protect Jewel, that's why. Because he was a knight, not a kid, that's why.

It was time for another leap of faith.

"Step back," he told Nate. Then he hurled his Sword across the darkness like a neon javelin. The glowing diamond blade clattered to the floor a dozen feet beyond the pit.

"What the—" Aaron began.

"I want to see how far I have to jump," Matterhorn explained. The butterflies in his stomach had been swallowed by seagulls. Maybe if they all flapped at once, they would lift him over the chasm.

"Since I met you," he grumbled to the Baron, "I've had to jump out of a burning building, dive off an 800-foot waterfall, and now leap over a bottomless pit."

The Baron grinned. "Exciting, isn't it!"

Matterhorn had to admit it was—but not out loud.

"Haven't got all night!" Nate shouted, giving the rope a tug.

"You can do it," the Baron encouraged.

Matterhorn crouched like a sprinter and rocked back and forth in his stance. Twice, three times, then he shot forward on adrenaline-powered legs.

His jump would have set a record if it had been done at a high school track meet rather than in a sealed tomb. He landed less gracefully than Nate had, but scored the jump a "10" anyway.

The Baron also made it across, but banged his left knee in the process. Matterhorn helped him up, collected the Sword, and started after Nate. The trail of footprints led them to a T-intersection and a stunning piece of stone artwork. The facing wall was tattooed with men and animals, all haloed with blue, green, and red sun disks. At its base they saw the back half of a footprint.

"Moccasin," Nate said.

"Jewel," Matterhorn agreed, stooping to examine the heel mark.

The Baron put his ear to the wall and rapped hard with his knuckles. "It's hollow behind there. This slab must have slid into place after she passed. Maybe we can force it back."

They put their shoulders to the stone and strained to shift it out of their path, with no success.

"We'll never budge this thing," Matterhorn grunted.

Nate began feeling his way down the narrow hall running parallel to the wall.

"Where are you going?" the Baron asked.

"Builders sometimes hid emergency exits near traps in case they got caught themselves," Nate explained. "Bring the light."

Matterhorn and the Baron joined the search. Soon, Aaron's keen eyesight caught a thin crack around a three-foot stone near the floor. He pushed one side with his foot. It pivoted a few inches on a central pin. Dropping to his knees, he revolved through the opening and began yelling for Jewel.

"Over here!" she cried from a chamber to his left.

Matterhorn spun through the slot and hurried after the Baron. They found Jewel in a small room full of model boats and dismantled chariots. Various weapons were stacked atop tall wooden boxes. Jewel sat on the floor in a tiny pool of moonlight petting a cream-and-chocolate-colored cat. The milky glow came from a long, slanted vent in the opposite wall.

"Are you okay?" the Baron asked.

"The poor thing must have fallen down that shaft," Jewel said, not thinking of the worry she had caused her friends. "It's been in here for days; it's just fur and bones."

The Baron looked at the cat in Jewel's lap: its front paws extended sphinxlike, its regal head held high. He couldn't tell how skinny the animal was and he couldn't care less. "You risked getting killed for a cat!" he sputtered, his relief souring to sudden anger.

Jewel bristled. "How would *you* like starving to death?" Right away she regretted her sharpness. "I'm sorry," she apologized. "It was dumb to go wandering away. Thanks for coming after me."

"If you've finished your, er, business," Nate said awkwardly, "we should get back."

"What about the wall?" Jewel asked, getting to her feet.

"It's not going anywhere," he replied.

"But we are," Matterhorn said, leading the way.

While waiting for the others to squeeze through the small door in the side passage, Matterhorn noticed a gleam not far from where he stood. "What's that?" he wondered aloud.

"None of our business," the Baron replied.

But Matterhorn was already heading for a closer look.

The glint came from a gold collar—draped around the neck of a corpse!

Winepress

THE stench was gone but bits of loose skin still hung on the macabre face. Skeletal limbs rested beneath the rotting linen of the man's ragged clothing. He had most likely been a grave robber because he had several beaded necklaces and jeweled pendants strung across his bony chest. An inlaid silver box overflowing with rings, scarabs, and amulets, rested against his exposed ribcage. Precious stones had spilled out like pieces of a broken rainbow.

What had actually been broken were the man's legs. A large stone had crushed everything below his pelvis.

Nate pointed to a gaping cavity in the ceiling. "Another booby trap."

The gruesome scene made Jewel even more aware of how foolish she had been. "I've seen enough of this house of horrors," she said with a shiver.

Matterhorn lit the way back through the gallery hall. When they reached the chasm of missing floor, Jewel gasped. "How did this get here?"

Nate explained the trap and nixed the idea of looking for another route. "Too dangerous. Known hazards are easier to handle than hidden ones."

The Baron's bruised knee, and Jewel's flat refusal to try, meant they couldn't leap the abyss like last time. Fine with Matterhorn; his tired legs felt as wilted as week-old celery.

"If we can't fly," Nate said, "we'll walk." He looped one end of their rope under Matterhorn's arms and with the Baron's help, lowered him into the hole.

The pit only seemed bottomless. After a descent of twenty feet, Matterhorn reached the floor. It creaked under his weight and shifted slightly. He released the rope and it came down a minute later wrapped around Jewel. She cradled the cat, who was not too thrilled about what was happening.

The floor sank another inch.

Had one of the walls just moved?

"You better hurry," Matterhorn shouted into the darkness above. "This place isn't stable!"

The Baron came next, but instead of untying himself he pulled the rope down into the pit. That's when Matterhorn realized no one was left to lower Nate. How would the bushman get down?

A moment later, Nate landed in front of Matterhorn as lightly as if he'd hopped from a curb onto the street. The emeralds in the soles of his Sandals blinked brightly and then dulled to cool embers.

Matterhorn wanted to ask about the shoes, but two other matters suddenly became more pressing—the walls!

The floor had dropped enough to release them, and the reservoir of sand behind each was shoving them toward a pressing meeting in the middle.

"Get out!" Matterhorn yelled as he pushed Jewel forward. They scurried across the narrowing floor to the far end of the pit where Nate gave a further demonstration of the power of his footwear. Grasping one end of the rope in his teeth, he rushed to the corner and ricocheted upward from one surface to the other.

The Baron lassoed Jewel and a moment later Nate began pulling.

"Hurry!" Matterhorn shouted as he boosted Jewel and her feline companion upward. The sides of the deathtrap were closing!

"You next," urged the Baron when the rope came down.

Matterhorn shook his head. "Age before beauty; get in the noose!"

"No time to argue!" the Baron cried. He pushed the rope toward Matterhorn.

"Then don't!" snapped Matterhorn, shoving it back.

"Someone get up here NOW!" Nate roared.

The walls were less than four feet apart; time for one more escape. "Trust me," Matterhorn said. "I won't die down here."

His confidence gave Aaron the faith to take the rope to safety.

Matterhorn hadn't lied to save his friend. He drew his Sword and, turning it sideways, put the pommel against one wall just as the other wall crunched into the tip. He knew the Talis had been formed by the Maker and could not be destroyed. He glimpsed the familiar words on the silver crosspiece: *Truth is a Blade sharp as Light.* The truth was that the Maker would watch over His Talis and those who carried them. Matterhorn would stake his life on it.

He just had.

On both sides, the twin seas of sand pushed the walls forward. The Sword separating them, however, showed no signs of stress. The diamond encased light didn't bow or bend. The tip didn't dull. The silver pommel didn't dent. Once more Matterhorn found the Maker as good as His word. "Thank you," he whispered.

The walls at the other end of the pit came together. Nearer to Matterhorn they groaned and began to crack. He realized that while the blade would not bend, the stone would soon break."

"Toss me the rope!" he yelled upward. At once the Baron obeyed. Matterhorn tied the end around the hilt at the crosspiece, then hollered, "Pull up the slack!"

Nate and the Baron tugged cautiously at first, not wanting to dislodge the Sword.

Matterhorn tested the line and cried, "Harder, pull harder! The Sword's not going anywhere!"

Hand over hand, Matterhorn hauled himself up the rope. The Sword remained as firm as rebar in concrete.

Overhead, Nate's Sandals had become one with the floor. Jewel gently dropped the cat and squatted next to the pit. She grabbed Matterhorn's collar when he neared the edge and helped him out. The two toppled backward.

The crunching from below grew louder. Nate and the Baron strained at the rope, trying to free the Sword. "We could use some help," the Baron grunted.

"Let me," Matterhorn said, scrambling to join them. He took the rope and gave it a sharp jerk with his left hand. At the same instant he willed the Sword into travel mode. The blade retracted and he caught the hilt with his right hand as it flew out of the pit.

Supper Party

FEELING like trespassers, the Travelers put their senses on full alert and started walking single file with Matterhorn in the lead. When they got to the narrower corridor, Jewel saw who had been spying on her earlier. In the Sword-light she noticed two life-size wall carvings. They had the bodies of men and the dog-shaped heads of jackals. Red garnet pupils shone from their golden eyes.

"Anubis," Nate told her when she stopped. "Egyptians believe he's the god who escorts the dead to judgment."

"Garnet is my birthstone," Jewel said. "These are the biggest I've ever seen." She reached up and touched one of the perfectly round eyes.

Friends at home teased Nate about his big ears, but he could hear the beating of a mosquito's wings before it landed on his arm. He heard the tiny "click" overhead and realized instantly what the sound meant. He tackled Jewel sideways just as a large chunk of limestone crashed to the floor.

Another near-death experience, compliments of the tomb's designers.

As the dust swirled around them, Nate said, "If I let you up, promise not to touch anything?"

"Promise," Jewel coughed. She got up and found her cat, who glared at them from a corner. It had been fumbled down the hall like a furry football when Nate had tackled Jewel.

The weary party reached the storeroom without further incident and collapsed on the circle of carpets. Jewel poured water for their new mascot into her palm. It lapped up several refills and then purred over some small bits of jerky Jewel hand-fed her.

Matterhorn stretched out and studied the sleek animal. The round face was evenly divided by a long, thin nose. On either side budded an almond-shaped eye of neon blue. Slim legs ended in sharp claws. The tail tapered to a dark point that matched the tips of the triangular ears.

"I think I'll call her Cyan," Jewel purred. "Her eyes are so blue."

Nate reached over and stroked Cyan's silky coat. "Most breeds of domestic cats come from Egypt," he said. "This one looks like an ancestor of the Siamese."

Matterhorn preferred dogs. Seeing Jewel with Cyan made him miss Christy, the sheltie he'd gotten for Christmas a few years ago. And watching the cat chew the dried meat made him think of his own hunger. Patting his pockets, he found a few leftover pods from the volcano where they'd recently been. He split one open with his thumb and popped the olive-sized seeds into his mouth. He tossed another to the Baron.

"Uck!" Aaron said, swatting the pod away. He scrounged in his pack for anything edible.

Jewel picked it up and said, "These aren't that bad. I've had worse."

"Like what?" Matterhorn asked. "What's the most disgusting thing you've ever eaten?"

Jewel sucked on a seed and mused. "Raw salmon eggs," she finally said, wrinkling her nose.

"Rich people love fish eggs," the Baron said with his trademark laugh. "Ever hear of caviar? The worst thing I've ever had in my mouth was burnt caterpillar. It took hours to get the little legs from between my teeth."

"That doesn't count," Matterhorn protested. He threw a cushion at the Baron's head. "You didn't even swallow."

The Baron caught the cushion with one hand and put it behind his neck.

"Caterpillars are better raw," Nate observed.

"What about those Luwak berries you gave us this morning?" the Baron asked. "Were they really pooped out of a weasel?"

"Sure as truth," Nate said. "Luwaks eat coffee beans but can't digest them. When they come back out, they've got an extra enzyme kick." He padded a pouch on his belt. "Worth more than gold in some places."

That was more information than Matterhorn needed as he thought back to the brown berries he'd sucked on earlier. "I bet you've eaten some strange stuff in the bush," he said.

"You mean like witchetty grubs and mangrove worms? Or termites? Don't even have to chew the little buggers; they just crawl down your throat."

The Baron scraped his tongue on his teeth and said, "What about that pepper leaf you put on my food a few days ago? That was pretty awful."

"You're a food wimp," Matterhorn said. Then he asked Nate, "What's the most horrible thing you've ever eaten?"

"Worst tucker I ever had was peanut butter." Nate's face contorted as he licked the pasty memory from his mouth.

The Baron took a long drink and changed the subject. "You like playing Sherlock Holmes," he said to Matterhorn. "What have you deduced about our rescuer?"

"There's more to Elok than he lets on," Matterhorn replied. "His hands are strong but he doesn't have calluses from manual labor. Also, his fingernails are clean. And how many servants have time-sheets?"

"Maybe his master gave it to him," Jewel suggested.

"He was pretty adept at using it," Matterhorn said, rubbing his arm.

"Perhaps he serves a Praetorian," Jewel went on. "He looks more like a bodyguard than a servant."

"Praetorians don't need bodyguards," the Baron pointed out.

"He doesn't carry a weapon," Nate said, "and he's solid as a rhino."

"You bumped into him on purpose when you got here," Jewel said knowingly.

"Would you believe I tripped?"

"Not bloomin' likely with those Sandals," the Baron quipped, mimicking Nate's Aussie accent.

Matterhorn took a closer look at the metallic shoes. He searched for the Maker's handwriting that marked each Talis. There, across the hammered-gold strap, he spied the text: *Stand firm in Me and you will never fall.*

"Where can I get a pair of those?" Matterhorn asked.

"One Talis per Traveler, mate. Wanna trade?"

"No way," Matterhorn said. He reached over for the skinny neck of a ten-string lyre sticking out of an open chest. After breaking two strings trying to tune it, he resorted to his harmonica for some music.

Things got rowdy when Nate found a set of hand drums. The Baron joined the band as lead vocalist, using his switchwhip handle as a microphone and making up words about their recent adventures. His singing was like his cooking—well meaning but awful.

Jewel laughed so hard she had to hold her sides.

Cyan pretended to ignore the foolishness, but her tail told the truth as it kept time with the rhythm.

Never had a chamber of the dead been filled with such live music.

Dress for Success

MATTERHORN awoke before the others with no way of telling if it was day or night. The surrounding darkness was asphalt thick. He felt stiff between the shoulders and damp with sweat. He had been dreaming about playing goalie with his *shinai*, a kendo practice sword, and whacking midfielders when they came into the penalty box.

He could hear the Baron's soft snores and Jewel's rhythmic breathing nearby. Quietly, he stretched his arms as if making a carpet-angel. His right hand brushed something dangling from an open chest he'd pushed aside earlier. Curious, he pulled on the strand and out came a medallion about the size of a silver dollar. He felt some sort of pattern etched on one side.

He bit the edge of the metal, which yielded slightly to the pressure. It must be pure gold to be that soft! On impulse, he decided to keep the piece as a souvenir and put it around his neck. When he tucked the valuable medal into his shirt, it felt cool against his skin.

This wasn't stealing, he reassured himself, just taking a memento of his visit to Egypt. Wait till the guys at school got a load of this. He traced the pattern through his shirt and started to daydream—until his conscience raised a question.

The Baron had once told him that Travelers were not to interfere with the places they visited. Was pocketing a gold piece interfering?

This was a sealed tomb, Matterhorn's mind countered. No one would ever know the medal was gone.

Did this make him a grave robber?

Absolutely not! It was one lousy trinket. This place probably had more gold than Fort Knox.

At least ask the Baron if it's okay, the inner voice pleaded.

Not now. Maybe later when he . . .

A faint light fringed the doorway and distant footsteps broke the silence. Soon Elok's large bulk filled the opening. He held a torch and a jug of water in one huge hand. A wicker basket of bread and fruit hung from the other.

"Rise and shine," he bellowed cheerfully as he put the torch in a wall socket. "I see from the footprints in the hall that you ignored my warning." When he noticed the fur ball asleep next to Jewel, he added, "It appears that curiosity got the cat."

"Cyan," mumbled Jewel sleepily, "this is Elok. He's going to get us out of here. And soon, I hope."

Cyan stretched as only a cat can and dismissed Elok with a casual flick of her tail.

While the Travelers ate breakfast, Elok unslung a large shoulder bag and laid out a linen tunic for each. "These are workmen's garments," he explained. "They are the only people allowed into the valley."

"Because the pharaohs are buried here," Matterhorn said as he came over to finger the tightly woven fabric.

Elok nodded and took a stubby glass container from his bag. "Your faces need some work. You first." He motioned Matterhorn closer to the light, then dabbed a brush in the bluish-green paste and applied it to the top of Matterhorn's cheeks.

"What's that?" Matterhorn asked.

"*Kohl*. It is made from powdered lead and copper oxide. It reflects the sun and reduces eyestrain."

"I can do that myself," Jewel said when it was her turn.

Next came the wigs. Elok produced a hairpiece to cover the Baron's buzz-cut hair. "Your scalp will be blistered by midday without this." He touched his own wig tucked into his belt. "The Egyptians wear these like hats."

The Baron wanted to wear his red corduroy baseball cap, but that would have drawn more attention than walking around with a cobra on his head. He sighed and took the wig.

Elok also gave Matterhorn a hairpiece because his Irish setter ponytail would stick out like the Baron's cap. The Princess didn't need to cover her dark-chocolate hair. Neither did Nate. His thick wiry hair would protect him.

Elok gave them back their universal translators, along with a fabric bag for each. "Put your stuff in these," he instructed.

Nate declined a bag. He carried everything he needed in the kangaroo-skin bum bag nestled in the small of his back and in the tucker-bag hanging from his belt. His short mulga wood boomerang rested snugly against his left hip. Slipping a tunic over his khaki shorts and tank top, he pronounced himself good to go.

The Baron put his tunic over the light gray T-shirt and the faded cargo pants he always wore. Matterhorn donned his own white outfit, careful to conceal the medallion from the others. He was about to put his belt and Sword outside the tunic when Elok said, "Best keep that hidden."

Everyone except Nate exchanged their shoes for sandals made from plaited palm leaves. When they had finished dressing, Jewel said, "Nate's the only one who looks like he belongs in the desert."

"Nate the Nubian," teased the Baron, referring to Egypt's dark-skinned neighbors to the south. "And your permanent suntan will help you blend in, Jewel of the Nile."

"A gift from my father," Jewel said, rubbing both cheeks. She was proud of her cinnamon skin and Chinook heritage.

"Even you have a tan," Nate said to Aaron. "But Matterhorn's as pale as an albino rabbit."

"I can fix that," Elok responded. He began smearing rouge on the pink chin and cheeks beneath the *kohl*.

"Think of it as sunblock," he told a grimacing Matterhorn, whose face was reddening nicely on its own.

When they were ready, Elok led the disguised Travelers along the main corridor and through a maze of upward passages. On the way to the surface, he pointed out some of the deadly surprises they *hadn't* managed to trip the night before.

At last they climbed a narrow stairway to the landing in front of a stout door. Elok shoved it open with his hip. "Welcome to the Valley of the Kings."

East Side, West Side

A HOT desert breeze slapped the visitors and threw sand in their eyes. The last time they had seen the sun, it floated in fleecy clouds above a rain forest in North America. Now it glared angrily at them from an austere sky. Elok put on his wig while he waited for the others to regain their sight. He looks different in a hairpiece, Matterhorn thought. Less sinister. Still, not the kind of man you would ask for directions.

Elok led the way with the grace of a big cat, never losing his footing on the narrow path Father Time had chiseled into the steep limestone cliffs. The sparse terrain seemed a fitting place for the dead. Not even the rumor of a tree or plant appeared in the bleak landscape.

Jewel shielded Cyan's face and scanned from one horizon to the other. "Where are the pyramids?" she asked.

"Far to the north in Giza," Elok replied. "The tombs here are carved deep underground. Still, there is *el-Qurn*."

He pointed back to a pyramid-shaped mountain tower-
ing a thousand feet above where they walked.

Guards peered down from their perches on top of the
cliffs but did not challenge the group as they headed out
of the valley. After winding eastward for twenty minutes,
they caught sight of the green floodplains of the Nile.

Across the river sprawled a thriving metropolis of
mud brick houses, brightly painted palaces, and elaborate
stone temples. "That's Waset," Elok said, "better known
as Thebes." He lifted his wig and wiped the sweat from
his scalp before nodding to the foreground and adding,
"This is the necropolis."

"City of the Dead," the Baron translated as he began
counting the temple complexes crowded together on the
riverbank. The necropolis comprised four square miles
of funerary business, at the southern end of which sat a
small village.

"*Deir el-Medina*," Elok said. "The stoneworkers,
plasterers, and painters live there."

"I don't suppose we can look around a bit," the
Baron said.

"We must cross the river. Kyl is waiting."

"Your master?" Jewel asked.

"Yes. Now hurry or we will miss the ferry." He
herded his charges through the busy temple area to the
docks, and soon they were barging across the Nile.

Matterhorn noticed sleek fishing eagles patrolling
overhead. Flocks of light pink flamingos played in the
water, careful to avoid the lethargic crocodiles and massive hippos lolling near shore.

The Baron tracked Matterhorn's wide-eyed wonder and said, "Some scholars think those animals are the Leviathans and Behemoths of old. Grand beasts, are they not?"

Matterhorn had to agree.

When the barge reached its destination, the Travelers joined the bustling throngs of Egypt's crown city. The home of pharaoh—and 50,000 of his subjects—Thebes stretched like an oblong oasis along the eastern floodplain. Buildings of every kind sprouted among the plush greenery. Colorful gardens flanked the houses. Fields of barley and flax flourished in the near distance.

A steady stream of foot and animal traffic flowed along the wide avenues and swept the newcomers through open markets and crowded bazaars. Their U-Trans buzzed with the haggling of merchants, the complaints of servants, and the latest gossip about the royal family.

Matterhorn marveled at how casually the people mingled with each other. Government officials and priests rubbed shoulders with scribes and soldiers. Farmers and laborers of both sexes milled about everywhere. No one seemed in much of a hurry.

They passed a number of temples, each fronted by rows of ornate columns. Matterhorn longed to go exploring, to peer inside the sacred structures. With such beautiful exteriors, what glories must lie within! Perhaps after their meeting with Kyl they could take a more leisurely tour of Thebes.

But only after the sun went down. The oppressive heat made him feel like a broiled chicken by the time they stopped at a two-story stone house. Large windows and a shaded wraparound porch gave the place an inviting air. A well-fed canal kept the side gardens green and lush.

Inside the house a servant greeted them with water and fig cakes. Another washed their feet, as was the custom in the East. Then Elok led them into the richly appointed main hall, or *qa'a*, where a man sat on a low stool surrounded by an assortment of cushions and pillows.

"Always a pleasure to meet Travelers," their host said. "Thank you for coming. My name is Kyl."

Kyl was not as big as Elok, but his presence was more commanding. A milk-white tunic with gold embroidery hung loosely on his broad frame. Below its hem were tan calves that seemed carved from oak. Brown hair and a well-trimmed beard and moustache accented his blue-eyed, leading-man looks. He wore a U-Tran similar to theirs.

The Baron introduced himself and the others.

"Pleased to meet you," Jewel said. "This is Cyan."

Nate said, "G'Day."

Matterhorn offered a "Yell-O."

Kyl gave him a questioning look and asked, "You are the one who carries the Sword of Truth?"

Matterhorn reached beneath his tunic and brought out the red leather hilt. The double-edged diamond blade extended of its own accord and pulsed with light. "I was called by the Sword to help recover some of the Talis,"

Matterhorn said. "That's what we were doing when Elok rescued us from the wraiths."

Kyl nodded, having been briefed by Elok. "The Queen knows of your quest?"

"She's the one who sent us," Matterhorn said.

"We have been away from the Realm for a time. Tell me of the Queen, is she well?"

"She is new to the throne," the Baron replied. "Her father was murdered not long ago."

"So I had heard," Kyl said. "How is she managing her new responsibilities?"

Matterhorn shrugged. "I've only been to First Realm once. But I've seen her twice on Earth. She's a courageous woman."

"And a bit stubborn," the Baron mumbled.

This remark raised Kyl's eyebrows.

Aaron shifted uneasily. "Elok told us you're a royal. What brings you to Egypt?"

"Make yourselves comfortable and I will explain."

Tut-Tut

THEY arranged themselves on deliciously fat cushions while a clap from their host brought servants with trays of honeyed fruits and nuts. "How well do you remember Egyptian history?" Kyl asked when the servants had gone.

"Let's see, Egypt was the first great empire," Matterhorn said. "She conquered her neighbors and ruled the Mediterranean world until the Romans."

"What do you remember about Pharaoh Tutankhamen of the eighteenth dynasty?"

"You mean King Tut?" the Baron replied. "I've seen pictures of his mummy. He was the greatest pharaoh of them all. He established a written legal code and built trade routes to the Near and Far East."

"Founded the greatest library in the ancient world here in Thebes," Nate said, being careful not to drip honey on his tunic. "Made this city the center of a golden age of learning." Nate was a history buff and probably knew more about Egypt than anyone in the room.

"And how did King Tut die?" Kyl asked.

"Old age," Nate replied. "He was in his eighties. Elok said this is 1325 BC. That would put us early in Tut's reign."

"Actually, it is the end of his reign," Kyl said softly.

"Can't be," Nate disagreed. "Tut doesn't even set up the Nile Peace Alliance until 1310 BC." Nate could understand these recent arrivals being mistaken about Earth history.

"That international alliance will never be formed," Elok said. "Tutankhamen was murdered last week at the age of nineteen."

"What!" the Baron said, louder than he intended. "I'm positive he lived to be an old man. How else would he have had time to build the great canals or do the other things that made him famous?"

"All that is gone now," Kyl said. "Erased. Check the history books when you return home. And no one on Earth is aware that history should have been otherwise— except you four."

The Baron nodded slowly. "That's why you're here?" he said. "It's started."

"Yes," Kyl said.

Matterhorn realized what the Baron meant. "The heretics!" he blurted. "They're hijacking our history!" A cold front of panic blew into his chest and slowed his heart.

"How are they able to travel without using the Propylon?" Aaron asked.

"Traitors among the Praetorians may be helping them," Elok said. "Or perhaps they have stolen the Traveler's Cube."

"You can scratch that last guess," the Baron said, producing the Talis Queen Bea had committed to his care.

Elok looked both relieved and concerned by this revelation. "The heretics may have a time-sheet," he went on. "We are not certain."

"That could explain how they sent wraiths after the Band of Justice," Jewel said.

"And how they sent one to fetch Ian's Flute," the Baron added.

Kyl sat up straight at the news. "What is this about Ian's Flute?"

The Baron and Matterhorn took turns telling about their first adventure, starting with their meeting in the Royal Chamber of the Propylon. Matterhorn explained how he had been pulled through a most unusual book and dumped at the feet of Queen Bea. After swearing allegiance to the Maker and the Sword, he went with the Baron to Ireland.

Aaron went on to tell of finding Ian and Bonehand, of tracking the thief Karn to the Irish coast and of fighting pirates, whose captain turned out to be a wraith. He ended by saying, "If Matterhorn hadn't slain the dark spirit we wouldn't be sitting here now."

Matterhorn winced at a phantom pain in his thigh where he'd been stabbed during the battle on the beach. The wound had healed but the memory remained sharp. "I didn't kill the wraith," he clarified. "It was the Sword."

"Your humility is fitting," Kyl said. "But do not sell yourself short. Surviving an encounter with a wraith puts you in rare company." He folded his hands and touched his fingers to his chin in a show of respect.

The Baron continued their tale. "One of the animals we rescued—a unicorn—turned out to be the Queen. She risked her life to help us, and together we recovered the Flute. She took it back with her."

"The Queen takes too many chances," Kyl said with a note of concern.

"Reminds me of her father," Elok said. "Rest his soul."

Suddenly a ball of fur flew through a window and threw itself at Kyl's neck. The blur resolved into a long-tailed green monkey. He bared his sharp teeth and hissed at Cyan, who until that moment had been resting quietly. The cat leaped into the air and wrapped herself around Jewel's head like a turban with claws.

"Behave yourself, Jeeter," Kyl scolded. "This house came with a whole zoo of animals. This one is my favorite."

The monkey had olive green fur that lightened to gray on his underbelly and lower limbs. A band of white hair ran across his forehead and down the sides of his dark face. Large eyes studied the strangers from beneath thin pink lids.

Nate made a clicking sound with his tongue and held open his palm with a single Luwak berry in it. Jeeter darted over to Nate's lap and snatched the prize. Cyan came down from her perch but kept her distance.

Kyl wiped monkey slobber from his neck. "The story of the Flute tells me how you two got together." He shifted his penetrating gaze to Jewel and Nate and asked, "Where do you fit in?"

Jewel explained how Bea had appeared in a dream, had sent her to find the Band of Justice, and of how Nate had joined the search party. She calmly mentioned earthquakes and floods and narrow escapes. She related their capture by the wraiths and the forced march to the portal that ended with Elok's timely appearance.

Elok added his now familiar chorus. "It was the Maker's timing, not mine. He brought you here as surely as He did us."

"And how was that?" the Baron asked.

The rays of the afternoon sun had made their way across the room to the east wall by now. "Our story is boring compared to yours," Kyl said. "It is late and the telling would put you to sleep." He had noticed Jewel's yawning and Matterhorn's drooping eyelids. "You are weary from your ordeal. You should go home now and rest."

Kyl helped the Baron up and while still gripping his arm said, "The Traveler's Cube would be of great help in stopping the heretics. Allow Elok to take you home and keep the Talis."

The Baron shook off Kyl's hand. "Queen Bea gave it to me," he answered. "She can ask for it back, but no one else. And as for going home, forget it. I'm staying." He looked around at his companions and said, "If anyone wants to leave, I'll take you."

It had been days since Matterhorn had seen The Loft in his backyard. Had his parents come out to check on him? What would they do if he weren't there? "How much time has passed at home since I've been gone?" he asked.

"It's relative," the Baron replied. "You should know that by now. I can return you within a few minutes of when we left."

Matterhorn put his hand on his Sword hilt and said, "No hurry, then. I'll stay."

Nate simply nodded to Kyl.

Jewel added a "Me, too," as she backhanded another yawn.

Kyl and Elok exchanged a knowing glance. "Very well," Kyl said. "The servants will prepare your rooms." He reached out to take Jeeter from Nate.

By now the monkey had stuffed several Luwak berries into his cheek pouches and was wound tighter than Nate's hair. When the bushman released him, Jeeter skittered up the walls and swung from tapestry to tapestry as if they were trees, chattering at the top of his shrill voice.

"What did you feed him?" Kyl asked.

The Baron cleared his throat. "You don't want to know."

History Channel

THE bedrooms proved as lavish as the rest of the house. The sky blue ceilings had flecks of silver that glittered like stars at night. The chairs and beds were lion-footed. Copper fittings capped the bedposts, and vases of hammered silver sat on calcite tables. Any one of these common household articles would have made a museum curator flush with pride.

Matterhorn shared a room with the Baron while Jewel had one farther down the hall. Nate preferred to sleep outside. Aaron sat down cross-legged on one of the thinly padded beds and began playing with the Cube. When he had the Talis aligned just so, he placed it carefully in front of him. With a scritching sound, he opened a pocket and pulled out a slim black device, which he aimed at the colorful Cube.

"What's that?" Matterhorn asked, propping himself on one elbow.

"My PDA."

Matterhorn stared at the gadget. "I've got a personal digital assistant, too. But what good will that do here?"

"I want to do some research on the Internet about what Kyl and Elok told us."

"How can you do that? The Net won't exist for thousands of years."

"I'll log on from the computer in my workshop," the Baron said. "When I started traveling, I figured a way to create a quantum uplink with my home computer. I can send a bit-stream from the infrared port on my PDA through one computer to the other and access the Net."

Matterhorn watched his partner touch an icon on the small screen. In a few moments information from the future scrolled into view. From a Web site about ancient Egypt they learned King Tut had died under mysterious circumstances before age twenty. His trusted advisor, Aye, had become Egypt's next pharaoh.

The Baron whistled. "Kyl will certainly be interested in that." He checked several more sites until a knock outside their curtained doorway broke their concentration. "Just a minute!" he yelled as he shut down the PDA and put it away. "Come in."

Two women entered, one carrying a shallow tray heaped with roasted duck swimming in onion broth, the other with a spread of rolls, dipping sauces, cheese wedges and a pitcher of dark liquid. After the ladies bowed out, the Baron and Matterhorn attacked the meal like piranha, leaving nothing but bones.

Between bites they discussed their situation. "What if Elok's time-sheet transported us to another version of reality," Matterhorn managed through a mouthful of fowl. "Maybe history is different because we're in a parallel universe."

"Nope," the Baron said. "If other universes exist, they couldn't interact with this one."

"What about First Realm?"

"It's part of this reality."

The Baron started to dip a corner of bread into a white sauce when Matterhorn warned, "That's a pretty potent horseradish. You might want to try a different color."

The Baron pulled his hand back.

"Should we go tell Kyl what we learned about Aye?" Matterhorn asked, licking his fingers.

"In a minute," Aaron replied, lying back to savor his supper. "I'm still not sure what to think about him and Elok. When they got here and saw they were too late to save King Tut, why didn't they return to the Propylon and come back a few weeks earlier?"

"That's a good question," Matterhorn said as he reached for the last of the cheese. He stretched out on his bed to give the matter some serious thought.

The next thing either of them knew it was morning.

A basin of water and two towels had replaced last night's dishes on the table between the beds. After a quick wash, Matterhorn and the Baron made their way toward the sound of breakfast. They found a meal of cool melons and warm flatbread already in progress.

The Baron told Kyl about surfing the Net and discovering the identity of the next pharaoh. Kyl was eager to learn all about Aye. Elok wanted to know how the Baron had created a stable data pipe and asked to see the PDA.

Kyl leaned back in his chair and stroked the furry animal by his side. Jeeter busied himself with a bowl of dates. The monkey was much calmer today, his red eyelids being the only evidence of last night's berry binge.

The Baron was about to ask his question from the night before when Jewel cut in. "I don't mean to be nosy, but if you recently came from the Realm, how did you get all this stuff? There are enough riches in this house to suit a sultan." She picked up a solid silver knife and used it to point at various objects.

"I came to Thebes with the means to set myself up as a wealthy merchant," Kyl answered. "I had hoped to be invited to the royal court where I could warn the pharaoh. He was killed before that happened. Today I will pay my respects to his widow and warn her of the danger she yet faces."

"Killing Tut was done to clear the way for another pharaoh," Elok said. "Whoever sits on his throne can help the heretics establish a beachhead from which to affect the rest of history."

"While the future reveals Aye will be the next pharaoh," Kyl went on, "we do not know if that means the heretics succeed in their plan or that we are able to stop them."

Jeeter pawed his way onto the table as Kyl spoke. His long tail caught the stem of a goblet and sent it tumbling to the floor.

Matterhorn did not see Kyl move, yet a second later he had the glass in his hand. Sitting it back on the table, he asked, "Would you like to come to the palace with me?"

"Good catch," Jewel said. "We'd love to go."

Kyl nodded. "You will find nicer clothes in your rooms along with the necessary makeup. On the hall table is a chest of jewelry. Help yourself."

Walking to their rooms a few minutes later, the Baron said, "Did you see Kyl catch that glass?"

"Quicker than a mongoose on a snake," Nate offered.

At the jewelry table, Matterhorn and Jewel pawed through earrings, necklaces, anklets, and rings. The Baron shook his head. "I'm not much for trinkets."

"When in Egypt, do as the Egyptians do," Jewel said, handing him a bracelet. She selected a beaded necklace that went with the onyx wolf earring she always wore in her right ear.

Back in the room, Matterhorn rouged his cheeks and applied *kohl*. The goo reminded him of the inky paste worn by ballplayers. He put on his wig and checked his U-Tran. Wearing the device had become second nature. He patted the gold medallion under his sun-bleached tunic and dismissed the idea of displaying it as part of his outfit.

He didn't want to draw attention to his little souvenir.

Street Waif

AFTER passing Elok's inspection, the Travelers became the entourage of Kyl the merchant. The bright morning air carried the smell of fish from the Nile. The only living things in this country grew along its annually flooding banks. The other 96 percent of Egypt was brittle desert.

As they strolled the streets of Thebes, Elok explained that the pharaoh lived in a separate residence from his queen. However, Queen Ankhesenamen and the other nobles would be receiving mourners at Pharaoh's palace today.

Seeing everyone's fascination with the surrounding buildings, Elok said, "Thebes is crowded with temples. Each ruler tries to outdo his predecessor in decorating them." He motioned to a complex of buildings and shrines sprawled across acres of luscious landscape on their right. "Pharaoh Amenhotep III erected those majestic gates."

Matterhorn craned his neck upward. The brightly painted pylons stabbed sixty feet into the sky. Their top pennants ruffled in the breeze. He looked down quickly at the touch of a wet nose on his bare calf. The pleading eyes of a scrawny dog met his, but Matterhorn had nothing to give. He shrugged and held out empty hands. With a low growl, the dog slunk away.

It soon became obvious that the city had more dogs than people. Sleek dogs, fat dogs, friendly dogs, junkyard dogs. Groomed dogs on leashes and mangy mongrels on the prowl. No one seemed to mind all this canine company except Cyan. She hissed with contempt from her regal perch in the crook of Jewel's arm.

"It's okay, baby," Jewel purred to her pet. She smiled at the sense of superiority the feline projected. All the cats she knew had high opinions of themselves, but Cyan believed she was royalty and all dogs were scum. Jewel also sensed horses, gazelles, and other creatures on some of the larger estates they passed. But where were the camels?

When she asked the Baron about it, he said, "Camels won't make it to Egypt for centuries. I think the Romans brought them here."

"Is that true?" Matterhorn asked doubtfully. He turned to ask Nate about the animal known as the ship of the desert, but the bushman had vanished.

It startled the vigilant Elok to have lost one of his charges. "I will circle back and find him," he told Kyl.

"I don't think so," the Baron said matter-of-factly.

Kyl was intrigued. "Elok is very thorough."

"I'm sure he is, but Nate's harder to find than a shadow at midnight."

"Why did he leave?" Kyl asked.

"He likes to be alone. He has his own way of—"

Just then a slender Egyptian bumped into the Baron. This jostling came with the crowds and Aaron muttered an "excuse me" for the tenth time that morning. The youth shrugged and silently moved on.

It took the Baron a few moments to realize something was missing. His shoulder pack!

"Stop!" he yelled as he bolted after the thief.

Matterhorn ran after the Baron.

"Come back here!" Kyl shouted. When they didn't obey, he took after them with Elok and Jewel in close pursuit.

The thief slithered through the sea of humanity like an eel. The grab had been clean but not perfect. The tall foreigner was giving chase. No matter. With a burst of speed, the pickpocket disappeared between two fruit vendors.

The Baron's 20/10 vision locked onto his prey as he ran. He had a compelling reason not to lose sight of his property. The cheap pack held an object more valuable than all the gold in Egypt. More valuable than all the gold on Earth.

The Queen had allowed him to carry the Traveler's Cube and he did not intend to let some lowlife waltz off with it. He shot between the fruit stalls and into the alley as the Egyptian veered left down a side street. Through the next two turns, he closed to within twenty yards.

The crowds kept him from using a throwing star to slow down the crook. Their presence also kept him from shedding his tunic, which kept getting tangled in his legs. He wasn't used to running in a dress. He knew Matterhorn and the others were trying to keep up but he couldn't slow down.

At least we're headed west, he realized with a glimmer of hope. Sooner or later, the Nile would draw the finish line to this steeplechase.

The same thought also occurred to the thief, who hadn't expected a foot race. It was too hot to be bolting through town like a wild donkey. Maybe it was time to drop the bag and be done with it.

Not yet.

The stranger's desperation meant the pack held something valuable, something worth a little extra effort. Thankfully, this part of the waterfront was familiar territory and the dockside fish market just ahead included the perfect hiding place.

The pickpocket shot through the bustling bazaar and slid under the ragged curtains at the back of a large booth. Tossing the pack under a low table lined with fresh fish, the youth plopped down by a man expertly filleting a red-tailed catfish.

"What's your hurry?" he asked without missing a stroke.

Grabbing a knife and laying into a fat mullet, the eager worker panted, "I-I wanted t-to help with the morning catch." A quick face wipe with a dirty rag, a tattered leather apron thrown over the lap, a few fish guts splattered here and there, and the disguise was complete. The petty crook had been transformed into a professional fishmonger.

"How thoughtful," the man drawled sarcastically. He didn't believe a word. The kid had been nothing but trouble lately. Smart as a dolphin but lazier than a barnacle. Something stunk, and it wasn't yesterday's catch.

When the Baron charged into the open-air market, his heart sank into his sandals at the sight of hundreds of sun-dried faces.

They all looked alike to him.

Go Fish

FOLLOWING his first adventure with the Baron, Matterhorn had taken up kendo to learn how to handle a sword. If he had known that being a Traveler involved so much running, he would have gone out for track, too. The hardest part of chasing the Baron turned out to be staying upright. He couldn't understand why the footing was so treacherous—until he glanced down.

A dog's gotta doo what a dog's gotta doo, he realized grimly. Even in the city. He wished he had on his hiking boots instead of these open sandals. But this was no time to be squeamish. He guessed the Traveler's Cube was in the stolen pack and imagined what the Baron must be going through. A Talis quickly became part of you. Losing it would feel like having a limb amputated.

Darker, more selfish thoughts bounced around in Matterhorn's mind as he careened through the streets. How would they get home without the Cube? Not knowing the answer made him run faster. After what seemed like a half marathon, he finally caught up to

Aaron in the fish market. The place smelled like spoiled sushi. Gulls screeched overhead and made daring dives on the overflowing gutbuckets beside the stalls. Hawkers and barkers cried for attention.

"Glad you could make it," wheezed the Baron, when Matterhorn reached him. Matterhorn was too out of breath to reply.

Kyl, Elok, and Jewel arrived a minute later. Elok started to scold the Baron for his rashness but stopped when he learned the Traveler's Cube was in the missing pack. He scanned the shoppers who swarmed like smelt among the rows of booths. "It will be impossible to find the thief in this throng," he pronounced.

"Maybe not," the Baron said with a gleam of an idea in his eye. He straightened and pressed the small silver stud on the belt buckle under his tunic. This triggered the homing device in his pack—the same device that had helped Matterhorn rescue him from kidnappers in Ireland. And the same device he had used to track Broc when the noble horse fell under the spell of Ian's Flute.

Travelers were not to draw attention to themselves by using advanced technology, but in this case he had no choice. He listened for an electronic beep above the din of the crowd and as soon as he got his bearings, he shut it off. Then he followed the fading pulses to a fish stall.

Without stopping his deft handiwork, the owner said to his suddenly terrified assistant, "I believe you have some customers."

The Baron leaned over the low table covered with the morning catch and said angrily, "I want my pack."

The youth briefly thought of running, but the two large men standing on either side of the stall made escape improbable. Embarrassed at being caught, and fearful of being punished, the thief sat motionless.

"My name is Bahari," the owner said, laying down his knife and wiping his hands. He wore a blue scarf instead of a wig and had the perpetual squint of someone who lived outdoors. His fuzzy eyebrows were unevenly stitched to his oily forehead. Tiny white hairs poked out of his wide nostrils. His sausage lips were pinched at both ends. From the number of his chins—three—and the size of his belly, the fish business had been very good to him. As he rose to defuse the situation, a loud commotion broke out at a stall across the way.

"I give you work and this is how you repay me!" shouted a red-faced merchant to a lanky teen. The youth tried to squirm away but his accuser pinned his tunic to a display board with a cleaver used for beheading fish. "You think I didn't see you palm those coins, you ungrateful viper. I ought to—"

The enraged owner grabbed the lad's neck with his scaly hands as two soldiers arrived. One of them used the pommel of his sword to club the struggling thief to the ground. The other stepped on the boy's forearm and forced his clenched fist open with the point of his blade. Three gold coins rolled out.

The soldiers roughly jerked the youth to his feet, not concerned that his outer garment was torn off in the process, or that his hand was bleeding. He was hauled away to the jeers of the bystanders, who pelted him with fish heads.

Bahari's gaze shifted from the other merchant's problem to his own with a clear resolve not to involve the authorities. He spread his arms to take in his booth and said to the Baron in a syrupy voice, "What's mine is yours. Take what pleases your palate and let's have no such unpleasantness." He nodded at an amber dish of *botarikh*, expensive Egyptian caviar, while with his right foot he pushed the pack out from beneath the table.

The Baron squatted and checked the contents. When he found the Traveler's Cube he kissed the deformed shape and tucked it into a pocket under his tunic.

"Forgive us, strangers," Bahari said. "The fault is partly mine. Since my wife died I have not been able to keep as close an eye on the youth as I should." He dropped his arms and sighed. "This is not the first time there has been trouble. And if you report this"—he made a sawing motion over his left wrist—"they will cut off my daughter's hand."

That last statement stunned the Baron and the others.

Not the brutality of the punishment, but the revelation that the thief was a girl!

Reluctant Guide

THE Baron's anger melted as soon as he recovered his Talis. Now he was a bit embarrassed at having been fleeced by a female. Before he could say "Forget it," Kyl stepped forward and said, "Your daughter is a scamp. Yet judging by the chase she led us, she knows the city well. I have a better use for her talent than thievery. I will hire her as a guide for a few days."

Bahari's face lifted at the word "hire."

The girl began to protest but her father growled, "Silence!" He leaned toward Kyl. "Go on."

Kyl removed a gold bracelet and handed it to the merchant.

Bahari bit the band to make sure the proffered payment was genuine. With the business part of his nature satisfied, the father in him said, "How do I know she will not come to harm? Perhaps you mean to take revenge on her away from witnesses." He motioned his daughter up and draped a protective arm over her shoulder.

"We are not barbarians," Jewel said. "Your daughter will be safe with us." The sincerity in her voice and eyes put Bahari at ease.

His daughter shrugged out of his grip, clearly upset at being treated like a common servant. "And what if I don't want to go?" she said brashly.

"You should have thought of that before stealing the pack," her father said, making the sawing motion again. He wasn't heartless. He loved his daughter and hoped that this humiliating experience might change her ways.

"Yes, father," the girl mumbled as her tawny complexion reddened.

Matterhorn couldn't tell if the blush was remorse or anger. She had the cutest dimples and the whitest teeth he had ever seen.

Turning to Kyl, Bahari said, "Abby is at your service for three days, no more." To seal the deal, he pocketed the bracelet.

Abby shucked her apron and mumbled, "I'm sorry for the trouble father; I will do as you say." Her dark eyes sent a different message. They were as hard as olive pits and as black as the hair peeking from under her scarf.

Sorry for getting caught is more like it, Matterhorn thought. Still, a guide in this exotic city wasn't a bad idea.

Kyl didn't buy Abby's apology either. "Do not shame your father further by trying to trick us. Steal anything else, or fail to serve well, and we will see that he pays fourfold for your crimes."

Abby softened at this. Her father was all the family she had left; she didn't want to cause him more pain. "I understand. Where do you want to go?"

"To Pharaoh's palace," Kyl said.

Bahari started to speak but Kyl said, "I know the young pharaoh has gone west through the reeds. I want to pay my respects to his queen."

Abby pecked her father's cheek and put another "sorry" in his ear. She bent down and grabbed the back of her tunic, pulled it between her legs and tucked it into her waist sash. In one leap she cleared the display table and started back through the bazaar.

"This way," she tossed over her shoulder. She wanted to get away from the haughty glares and wagging tongues of the other merchants. The tale of her disgrace would make its way through the market faster than water through gills.

Jewel scooped up a handful of sardines for Cyan. Bahari waved away any attempt at payment. He just wanted these outsiders to go away.

When the Travelers caught up to their sulky guide, Jewel fell in step beside Abby. She figured the girl to be fourteen or fifteen. She had the lanky build of a tomboy, narrow body, long neck, and skinny legs. Bright orange toenails stuck out the front of her straw sandals.

Trying to make conversation, Jewel said, "You run like a gazelle."

"And I would still be running if I had gone south instead of west."

"It wouldn't have mattered. The Baron would have tracked you across the desert if necessary. You took something very important to him."

Abby snorted.

Jewel tried again. "Where do you live?"

"None of your business." To discourage more questions, Abby set a brisk pace toward the royal palace. These strangers must have just washed down the Nile if they didn't know where the Divine One lived. She could give them the slip a dozen places along the crowded avenues, but they would only return to her father and take out their wrath on him.

Matterhorn glanced at the pretty face in profile on his right. The girl was definitely fuming. To lighten her mood he joked, "You do the crime; you do the time." The jingle didn't rhyme in Egyptian and came across as scolding.

He tried again. "What kind of name is Abby?"

"It's what my friends call me," she said. "Don't use it."

Musical Entrance

THE sun reached the center of the cloudless sky by the time Kyl and company arrived at the royal palace. Inside the main gate they marveled at the shimmering ponds, lush gardens, and grand plazas. Fragrant shrubs outlined wide pathways to the stately buildings. Ancient acacias and flowering mimosas gave the grounds the feel of a park. Turtledoves cooed from patches of shade while pigeons—sky rats to the Egyptians—pestered people for food. Iridescent green bee-eaters flashed among the red and blue hibiscus.

Elok slipped away and returned with a palace guard. Kyl spoke softly as he slipped the man a silver ring. The soldier escorted them through the milling mourners into a large reception area. Gigantic columns lined the unroofed hall. Shaven-headed priests in white robes gathered in holy huddles while knots of nobles tied up the archway at the far end. Burly men in uniform prevented anyone from going farther.

Matterhorn gawked at the pavement beneath his feet, painted to resemble pools teeming with exotic fish. It made him feel like he was walking on water.

Abby ogled at the riches flowing by. Her fingers itched just being around all this jewelry. Elok laid a huge hand on her shoulder. "Do not even think about it little one."

The people looked pretty as peacocks, but were crowded together like chickens in a coop. While Elok searched for a higher-ranking guard, Matterhorn wiggled his way to a pillar and sat on its flanged base. His legs ached from running through Thebes. On impulse, he took out his harmonica and began playing a quiet dirge to the dead pharaoh. He covered the silver instrument with both hands so no one would notice.

As often happened, Matterhorn soon got lost in his music. He didn't notice when the volume increased and the conversations around him gave way to his strange melody. He didn't register the growing silence; nor did he see the soldiers until they completely encircled him. Then he stopped suddenly, embarrassed at becoming the center of attention.

When the commander reached for the harmonica, Kyl stepped in, not the least intimidated by the officer or his armed escort.

The man stared at Kyl from eyes set deeply in his skull. His permanently sunburned skin was the color and texture of a walnut. A thin white scar sliced down his left cheek. He didn't like being challenged, but decided not to make an issue of it when Elok strode up next to Kyl. "The Queen asks about the strange music," was all he said.

"The musician is with me," Kyl replied. "Since I have business with Her Majesty, I will take him to her."

"And just who are you?" The officer's hand moved to the stubby bronze sword at his side. His men circled closer.

"I am someone you do not want to upset." The threat sounded ominous and believable. The blue in Kyl's eyes hardened to gun barrel gray.

A veteran of several campaigns in the South, the officer had danced with death in the desert and didn't scare easily. But he had been in the military long enough to know real power when he heard it. Spinning abruptly on his heels, he snapped, "Bring your man and come along."

"Way not to draw attention to yourself," the Baron said as they followed the guards through the curious crowd.

Matterhorn knocked the spit from his harmonica and put it away. "True talent is hard to hide."

"Don't you mean hard to find?"

Jewel elbowed the Baron. "He got us into the throne room."

"That's usually not a good thing," Abby muttered. Still, she was excited, having never seen royalty before.

The throne room was at the south edge of the hall, directly in front of pharaoh's personal quarters. Its deep pile carpets absorbed their footfalls as they entered the vaulted chamber. The brightly painted walls starred

Egypt's most famous kings doing what they loved best—hunting. Ostriches, antelopes, and lions fled from the hungry hounds and their handsome masters.

Matterhorn spied the young Queen sitting under a blue-fringed canopy. Nubian servants fanned her and the elderly man seated to her left. The throne to her right was empty. Ladies-in-waiting stood ready to do her bidding, as did her bodyguards.

The commander approached the throne and dropped to one knee. "Your Majesty, I have brought you the source of the strange music."

The Queen beckoned the visitors forward. Being First Wife, she wore an elaborate headdress that framed her regal face. She had a firm mouth and a sharp chin, which stuck out all the more because of her ramrod posture. Thick makeup hid her youthful skin but didn't cover her sadness. She had been married to her half brother, Tutankhamen, when they were both children. Now she was a widow while still in her teens.

Abby knelt, as did Elok, who signaled the others to do so. Kyl, however, remained standing. The older man near the Queen said, "Show proper respect to the Lady of the Two Lands."

"That is what I am doing," Kyl replied. "I am of royal blood and will not dishonor my family by acting otherwise."

The Queen made a hand motion to dismiss the matter. Intrigued by the stranger's boldness, she asked, "What is your name? Where are you from?"

Kyl touched fingertips to chin and said, "I am called Kyl. My home is far from here. I came to warn your husband of a common enemy who threatens both our kingdoms. I am sorry I arrived too late to save him. Nevertheless, I can still help you, for you are in great danger."

"And how can you help me?"

"Grant me a private audience and I will explain."

"Impossible," snapped the elderly man. "Speak your piece now." His voice sounded as though it came from a rusty gearbox. He had a sharp face with high cheekbones and no lips. Thin silver hair fringed his polished scalp. A jeweled neckpiece covered his upper chest. A more telltale sign of his status hung unsheathed at his waist—an iron sword. The dull gray metal was more rare than gold in Egypt.

"What I have to say is for the Queen's ears alone," Kyl said. "Who are you to tell her what she can and cannot do?"

The man folded his arms and sneered. "I am Aye. As Royal Counsel, I'll decide if what you have to say is worth Her Majesty's time. Now speak up or get out."

Kyl stoically studied Egypt's next pharaoh, then bowed and said, "Good day."

Stickup

A S Kyl and his party started for the door, two guards blocked their way. "Let them go," Aye ordered. "Take your petty secrets back to where you come from. We don't need advice from outsiders."

"What about my music?" the Queen spoke up.

"Perhaps a private concert?" Kyl suggested.

"Get them out of here," Aye growled. "I don't want to see their faces at the palace again."

The Queen began to protest, but a sharp glare from Aye silenced her.

Matterhorn felt sorry for the young monarch. Did she know that mean old man would be the next pharaoh? The gaunt fellow gave him the creeps. Kyl had been smart not to trust him.

The armed escort caught the crowd's attention. People murmured, then openly snickered at how quickly the strangers had been dismissed from their royal audience. The unkind remarks had no effect on Kyl and Elok, but Abby reddened at the ridicule.

The commander of this dis-honor guard had not forgotten what had drawn the Queen's attention in the first place. As the group passed through the courtyard he slipped up and pressed the tip of his short sword into Matterhorn's back.

Quietly, so as not to alert Kyl or Elok, he spoke into Matterhorn's ear. "Hand over the instrument you played and you can leave with the same number of holes in your skin you came with." He inched the sword forward to press his point.

The man smelled several days behind in his bathing. His breath stank of rotten teeth. Matterhorn felt more anger than fear at the sudden stab of pain. "Don't hurt me," he said as he reached under his tunic. "I've got something you'll like even better."

He faced the soldier and held out a red leather handle. Before the man could figure out what he was looking at, a diamond blade extended from the hilt to his throat.

"I've had just about enough of Egyptian hospitality," Matterhorn said. "And as my Sword is twice as long as yours, I suggest you back off."

Seeing a weapon suddenly appear in Matterhorn's hand brought a swift reaction from the guards, who drew swords and leveled spears. Before this circle of death could tighten, Elok snatched two spears and cracked their holders' heads together. The Baron disarmed a third soldier with a forearm chop.

"Enough!" Kyl shouted in a tone that suspended the action. He put his face close to the commander's and said for all to hear, "Aye ordered you to let us go. What is the penalty for disobedience?"

The poor man tried to speak without moving his jaw. The blade at his neck looked clear as water but sharp as glass.

"Dismiss your men," Kyl said.

"Return to the palace," the officer ordered as a bead of sweat slid down his scar.

The guards picked up their fallen comrades and slowly backed away.

Elok grabbed the commander's collar. "You come with us. When we are safe, you will be, too." To the retreating soldiers he said, "Follow us and you will make this man's wife a widow."

No one doubted that this giant of a man could make good on his threat.

Matterhorn wished he knew how to turn his U-Tran off as the commander explained in vivid language how *no one* was to follow them or even *think* of reporting this incident.

The Egyptians became stiff as Buckingham guards as Elok marched their leader out of the gate and into the city.

"What was that all about?" the Baron asked.

"The man wanted my harmonica," Matterhorn said. "I didn't want to give it to him, so I offered my Sword instead."

"That was a foolish move," Kyl cut in. "If word of what happened reaches the right ears our identities will be known."

Matterhorn hadn't thought of that. As usual, he had acted on impulse. He felt the sting of Kyl's rebuke. "I'm sorry—"

"What is done is done," Kyl said over the top of Matterhorn's apology. "But do not be so hasty next time. A warrior must know how he will end a fight before he starts one."

He was no warrior, Matterhorn knew. He couldn't even keep his temper in check. But what could he have done differently? Give up his harmonica? It didn't belong in this era, and that would have been against the rules for Travelers. He would write Kyl's words in his quote book as a reminder to think first.

When they passed an outdoor butcher shop about a mile from the palace, Elok hung the commander on a meat hook by his collar. Then Elok bent the hapless man's sword around his ankles like a pair of leg irons. Sweeping the startled onlookers with a searing gaze, he warned, "Whoever helps this man will answer to me."

The ominous threat kept anyone from rescuing the struggling soldier for almost half an hour. It took another half hour, and three men, to unwrap the sword.

The commander didn't make it back to the palace until evening. That gave him plenty of time to plan how he would track down and kill the foreigners.

Girl Talk

THE Travelers were now uncertain of their where-abouts, but with Abby's help, they eventually found their way back to Kyl's rented house. On that afternoon walk, Abby puzzled over these unusual outsiders. Their noble-born leader had refused to kneel in the Queen's presence and had gotten away with it. The giant tossed men around like toy soldiers. And the pink-faced one had a mysterious music box and a marvelous sword that appeared and disappeared at his whim.

The soft-spoken lady with the kind eyes and gorgeous hair seemed the least intimidating of the group. When she worked up her nerve, Abby said to Jewel, "You people are strange. Are all foreigners like you?"

"No, why do you ask?"

"Only curious."

"I'm curious about something myself," Jewel said, sensing their guide might be softening. "Abby doesn't sound like an Egyptian name."

"It's not," Abby replied. "I'm only part Egyptian. My ancestors came here long ago after one of them rose to power in pharaoh's court. But the good times didn't last."

"What happened?"

Abby rubbed the back of her neck and said, "The people lost favor and were enslaved by the new leaders. They did hard labor for hundreds of years until they decided to leave Egypt."

"So why are you still here?"

"My great-great-grandmother Abigail married an Egyptian. He was a kind man and she chose to stay with him."

Before Jewel could ask another question, they turned a corner and saw Kyl's place. Cyan jumped from her arms as Jeeter started screeching and jumping up and down on the porch. The servants came out and saw to the customary foot cleaning.

Refreshed and indoors, Jewel took Abby's hand. "Come on. I'll show you my room. You can sleep there tonight."

Later, in the garden, as a gentle breeze joined the party for supper, the Travelers said nothing in Abby's presence that would give away their real reason for being in Egypt. A day of walking and an hour of feasting left everyone fatigued. The talk faded and they retired early.

Jewel put the lamp Elok had given her on a shelf near the window in her room. Underneath sat a fancy wooden gaming box with ebony sides and an ivory top divided into thirty squares. Abby began taking carved game pieces from the drawers.

"Those are beautiful," Jewel said.

"They are made from hippopotamus teeth," Abby said. Her rings clattered on the glassy board as she arranged the pieces. She wore eight in all, each a different shape and color. "Do you know how to play senet?" she asked.

Jewel shook her head.

"It's easy. I'll teach you."

Although tired, the girls played and talked for a long time. At first, about the guys. "Are you related to any of these giants?" Abby asked. At five foot two, she was dwarfed by the men.

"No. We are just traveling together on business."

"Tell me about them. The redhead with the music box and magic sword . . ."

"Matterhorn the Brave," Jewel replied, "is the Queen's knight. The Sword he carries is quite unique."

"He was certainly brave to resist the commander and his soldiers," Abby said. Or incredibly dumb, she thought.

"He's also intelligent and funny and—there you are." She changed subjects as Cyan entered the room and jumped into her lap.

"Watch the tail," Abby scolded as a piece fell to the floor. After replacing the token, she asked Jewel, "What about the man who chased me after I, ah, borrowed his pack?"

"The Baron's the smartest man I've ever met. He can make or fix anything. He's been all over the world."

"Is either man your boyfriend?"

"Well, they're my friends, but not in the way you mean. I think of them more like big brothers. Your father said you are an only child, right?"

"I had a little brother once. He died when he was four."

"I'm sorry," Jewel said. She watched Abby move a marker and tried to remember what to do next. "I have an older sister, but I don't see her much."

"You don't want to do that," Abby said as Jewel reached for a piece near the one Abby had shifted. "This would be better."

Jewel took a deep breath and tried to concentrate. The scent of shredded eucalyptus leaves in the bowl of warm water by her bed made her sleepy.

"The rich merchant and his bodyguard," Abby went on. "What about them?"

"I haven't known Kyl and Elok that long," Jewel said, "but I know they can be trusted."

"What did Kyl want to tell the Queen? Is she really in danger?"

"I'm afraid so."

"He was right not to say anything in front of Aye. The old weasel has been the power behind the throne for years. My father says his hands are stained with royal blood." Abby caught herself and put her hand to her lips. "Don't tell anyone I said that," she pleaded. "Our lives would be forfeit."

"I won't," Jewel promised.

The more they talked, the more they found they had in common, including family tragedy. "It must be terrible losing your mom," Jewel said after they finished their second game. "When did it happen?"

"About a year ago." Abby spoke so quietly that Jewel had to lean forward. "My mother took a river trip with some friends. A hippo rammed their boat. She couldn't swim." Abby broke into tears under the weight of the memory. She had carried the pain for so long and needed someone to share it with.

"I'm so sorry," Jewel whispered as she wrapped her arms around Abby and rocked gently from side to side.

"You want to know the worst part?" Abby sobbed. "I was supposed to go on that trip but father needed me at the market. I was so angry that morning, but having to work saved my life." Her anguish spilled out; there was no holding back. "Sometimes I wish I hadn't been spared."

Jewel's heart ached for her new friend. Without wanting to, she began to think about her own mother, near death with cancer. "I don't think I can handle losing my mom," she sighed. Soon, her tears were mingling with Abby's, and the two became sisters that night as they shared the pain of loss—past and future—and cried themselves to sleep.

An hour after Jewel's lamp went out, six black-clad figures glided barefoot across the porch and through the open windows. The servants were gone, so no one saw the ghosts cross the carpeted room where Kyl had entertained his guests. Pairing off, they slunk down the wide hallway toward the unsuspecting sleepers.

No Trespassing

THE first team of assassins silently parted the curtains to the nearest room and crept toward Kyl's sleeping form with daggers drawn. Unknowingly, they walked right past Elok, who wasn't in the other bed as they supposed. He slept next to the door with his face flat on the floor. Not because he was a good servant, but because he was a very good bodyguard.

Elok instantly awoke at the slight vibrations of the intruder's footsteps. In one fluid motion he gathered himself and pounced with the fury of a lion. He also roared like one, meaning to terrify the assailants and warn the household. Charging low and fast, he drove the startled men past Kyl and into the wall. His forearms flashed upward and sealed off two windpipes, ending the brief struggle.

Kyl dropped to the floor and rolled to the chair on which he had draped his clothes. Throwing on his tunic he headed for the hall. He knew Elok well enough not to bother looking back.

Elok's warning cry had roused Matterhorn and the
Baron. At first, Matterhorn didn't remember where he
was as he sat up in strange surroundings. The two sil-
houettes standing in the doorway didn't help. Black
scarves hid their faces, but their evil intent was crystal
clear.

The Baron reacted to the sudden danger by snagging
his pack and slamming it into the stomach of the nearest
man. The intruder doubled over and the Baron made a
desperate lunge for the man's knife. They fought on the
floor with the sharp blade slashing in search of warm
blood. It didn't care whose.

Matterhorn grabbed for the Sword hilt on the table
and fell out of bed. The attacker jumped on his back,
putting Matterhorn in what wrestlers call the "position
of disadvantage." Double disadvantage since his oppo-
nent had a dagger.

But Matterhorn had weapons of his own—an arsenal
of wrestling moves his brother Vic had taught him. As the
attacker raised his arm to strike, Matterhorn did a cut-
roll, leaned back and grabbed the man's other wrist. Then
Matterhorn jerked the arm downward and rolled forward
over it. At the same time, he extended his left leg and
pushed against the man's knee. A quick hip-heist through
to a belly-down and the Egyptian was pinned.

Now what? Matterhorn wondered as his mind caught
up with his body. This guy was still armed and dangerous. Using his forearm as a lever, Matterhorn pushed off
the man's chest and made another lunge for the Sword

on the table. As he grasped the hilt, the Egyptian squirmed free and scuttled for the door. The panicked assassin stopped in the opening just long enough to hurl his dagger before making good his escape.

The Sword blade extended and spun Matterhorn around to the left. He heard the dagger bounce off the diamond shaft. He felt the impact. So why did Matterhorn's chest burn as if he'd been hit? No time to check for blood; the Baron and the second attacker were still writhing in a death match.

Matterhorn didn't dare use the Sword on the tangle of arms and legs and sheets. As the combatants tumbled nearer, he got a hot idea. He willed his blade to heat up and slapped it against the darkest foot he could make out in the gloom.

The Egyptian howled in pain and lost his concentration. The Baron slammed the man's knife-hand against the bed frame and the weapon skittered away.

Matterhorn yelped as well, for he felt the searing pain in his chest again. And when the Baron turned to see why his partner had screamed, his attacker got away.

Bolting into the hallway, the man didn't see Kyl, who plowed into him like a bull tossing a matador. Several ribs cracked as the man smashed into the wall. Kyl kept running toward the two sinister shadows he saw nearing Jewel's room.

The intruders heard the noise behind them as they prepared to enter the third bedroom. Being discovered before they had a chance to finish their business left them two choices: fight or flight. One man ran. Diving head-first through the window at the end of the hall, he fled into the night. The other man spun and threw his knife at Kyl.

The bronze dagger whizzed by Kyl's left ear.

Cursing his hasty aim, the killer reached for the short sword on his hip. Before the blade cleared its sheath, Jewel burst out of the room screeching like a howler monkey. She landed on the man's back and clawed at his face.

The assassin's hands flew up to protect his eyes. He grabbed Jewel's flailing arms and yanked her over his head as if taking off his shirt. She dug her nails into his thick wrists and kicked at his chest on the way down.

The Egyptian raised his foot to smash her throat just as Kyl's fist caught his chin. Unable to free his hands, he could not defend himself. Two more quick punches put him down for the count.

Kyl helped Jewel to her feet. She pushed the hair out of her eyes and said, "Thanks." Then she stuck her head into the room and said, "Abby, you can come out now."

Abby came into the hall, arms wrapped tightly around her chest to keep her heart from popping out. She had never been so scared, or excited! Staring at the unconscious man with the bloody face, she thought, What have I gotten myself into!

Third Degree

KYL didn't bother chasing the fleeing assassins. He had enough prisoners to learn what he needed to know. Picking up the Egyptian, he headed back to Matterhorn and the Baron's room. In the hall near their door, Elok stood over three barefaced men huddled beneath a sputtering oil lamp. Two of them were still unconscious. A third sat with his arms crossed over cracked ribs and his face set like stone.

The Baron leaned against the doorframe holding a piece of torn sheet to the gash on his forearm. An inch lower and the dagger would have cut a major vein and made a terrible mess. He watched Kyl make his contribution to the pile.

Behind him, Matterhorn sat on the bed and stared down at the round wound on his chest. It matched the size of the medallion hanging around his neck. The light from the Sword of Truth had somehow superheated the metal and caused the burn.

Matterhorn's conscience had also been scorched. Taking the artifact from the tomb had been wrong. The light of truth had painfully exposed his theft and reminded him of his duty. A Traveler's privileges weren't to be used for personal gain. He thought back to when Queen Bea had given him the Sword. She had warned him that the Talis would not tolerate any form of deception. He now realized that included self-deception. How foolish he had been to think there was such a thing as "petty" larceny.

He gingerly took off the medallion and put it in his cloth pack, vowing to return it as soon as possible. Then he joined his friends in the hall just as Kyl squatted in front of the man with the crossed arms.

"You have done a stupid thing tonight," Kyl said with icy calmness. "Do not compound your folly by refusing to answer my question."

The Egyptian bristled with arrogance and spat on Kyl's chest.

Kyl nodded to Elok, who heaved one of the unconscious men over his shoulder like a sack of grain and strode away. Several moments later a cracking, splintering noise broke the silence.

It sounded like a leg being broken!

Or a spine being snapped!

Jewel and Abby had dressed and joined the group by now. Abby turned pale at the nauseating crunch.

Kyl never flinched.

Elok returned alone and, without a word, scooped up a second man.

Silence.

Then the sickening sound effect repeated itself.

When Elok came back, he reached for the prisoner in front of Kyl. The terror-stricken man broke down and begged for mercy.

Kyl laid a restraining hand on Elok's arm. "Who sent you?" he asked the Egyptian.

"He will kill me if he learns I've told you!"

Kyl simply shrugged. Threats are unnecessary when it is clear that consequences are swift and certain.

As Elok yanked the man into the air, he shrieked, "All right, all right! Sebek sent us!"

"And who is Sebek?"

"He's the high priest of Amun-Ra."

"Where can I find him?"

"He serves at Karnak Temple."

This confession didn't prevent Elok from hauling the screaming victim away. The yelling stopped suddenly and everyone except Kyl cringed in expectation of the terminal crack.

It never came.

Jewel finally found her tongue. "How could you let Elok kill those men in cold blood?" she demanded.

"Bring this last one and I will show you." Kyl took the oil lamp from its hook and led them to his room. There they saw the three men Elok had carted off, bound and gagged and very much alive. Beside them on the floor lay a wooden chair—with two broken legs.

"Killing people seldom accomplishes anything good," Kyl said. "Besides, it changes the pattern of history, which is the very thing we are trying to prevent." Motioning Elok to follow, he stepped into the hall for a private conference.

Matterhorn and the Baron added their captive to the others and used the bed sheets to mummify the whole bunch. Abby aimed a foot at the closest prisoner's face but Matterhorn grabbed her ankle. "Don't kick a man when he's down, even if he deserves it."

"They would have slit our throats!"

"Returning violence for violence is stooping to their level," Jewel said.

"But how can you—"

Elok stuck his head in the room and ordered, "Come with me." They trudged back to the main hall where Kyl was busy stuffing items into a leather bag. Without pausing he said, "Some of the assassins got away and could return with more men. We must leave at once."

Safe House

Chapter 19

WHERE are we going?" Matterhorn asked.

Kyl glanced at Abby and paused. He wanted to go to the tomb in the Valley of the Kings, but not with her. He would release Abby from her obligation, take her home, and then cross the river. But before he could explain his intention, Abby piped up, "We can go to my house. It's near the market. We'll be safe there."

Staying there made more sense than trying to find passage across the Nile in the middle of the night. Kyl accepted the impromptu offer. "But only for tonight. Tomorrow we will find other lodgings and you can remain with your father."

Abby didn't want to be left behind. Yes, she had been frightened earlier, but this had also been the most thrilling day of her life. Since being forced to join this amazing band, she had been to see the Queen, had witnessed thieving soldiers put in their place, and had almost been slain in her sleep. She did not want to go back to gutting fish tomorrow.

"You'll still need a guide," she protested. "Thebes is a big place. You might get lost."

Kyl stopped packing and laid a hand gently on her shoulder. "When I hired you, I did not intend to put you in danger. I no longer need your services. I know how to find Karnak Temple."

Abby's face brightened. "If you're going to Karnak, you'll need me even more! My uncle's a stonemason. He spent a lot of time working at the temple. I played there as a child. I know it like a spider knows its own web, including how to get in without being seen."

She held her breath and waited.

Kyl resumed packing. "We are wasting time," he said. "Collect your things and be ready to go in five minutes."

Abby fumed at being ignored. She stomped her foot and insisted, "I can go anywhere I want!"

"No, you cannot," Kyl said.

"Yes, I can!" she fired back, lifting her chin and straightening her back.

"Not if you are helping us get into Karnak."

As they left the house minutes later, Kyl tossed a small bag of gold on the table to cover the damages and to pay for Jeeter. The monkey perched on his shoulder while he made everyone wait on the porch for Elok's "all clear" signal from the street. Jewel used the delay to dress the Baron's wound.

The city slept as they made their way westward. When they arrived at Abby's, she had to pound on the door for a long time to rouse her father. He became wide awake, though, as she said, "Some men tried to kill us. Others may try again. I told my friends they could hide here."

Bahari cursed under his breath. How had these foreigners become his daughter's friends in so short a time? And who wanted to murder them? The bloody bandage on the Baron's arm meant this was no joke. "Did anyone follow you?" he asked nervously.

"No," Elok said.

"Then come in." Bahari stepped back and opened the door. "My home is yours."

And quite a home it was. The sprawling, single-story house was almost as large and richly appointed as Kyl's rented mansion. Three wide corridors led off from the vaulted entry hall, which was frescoed with Nile scenery. Wooden pillars with detailed capitals supported the ceiling.

Bahari led the men to the left while Abby took Jewel straight ahead to her room.

The sheer elegance of the place startled Jewel. Beautiful hangings softened the walls and complimented the rich bedspreads and furniture coverings. Four narrow windows let in the cool breeze off the river. A shelf full of figurines cast miniature shadows above the largest bed, where Abby plopped down and kicked off her sandals. Long glittering necklaces of amethyst, carnelian, jasper, and onyx beads were casually draped around twin gold statuettes of Isis, the wife of Osiris.

Cyan began jumping and swatting at the dangling stones, which made the tired girls giggle.

Elegant quarters for a pickpocket, Jewel thought as she prepared for bed for the second time that night.

Lying a few feet from Abby after lights out, she asked quietly, "Why do you do it?"

"Do what," Abby said sleepily.

"Steal. You're obviously not poor."

"I'm not poor," Abby agreed.

"Then why?"

The answer was quick and unexpected. "To get caught." After a pause, Abby added, "And punished."

"But—"

"I shouldn't be alive while my mother and brother are dead," Abby interrupted in a quivering voice. "I don't deserve it."

Jewel swung her feet off the bed and sat up. Now she understood the false guilt that drove Abby to dangerous behavior. "The Maker assigns everyone a day to be born and a day to die," she explained. "We can't change that, and we can't walk another person's path."

"It's not fair!" Abby cried.

Jewel responded with the most comforting truth she knew. "Life's not fair, but the Maker is good. And He doesn't make mistakes. Your mother's work on Earth was finished. Yours is not. Perhaps He spared you so you could help us."

"But which god is the Maker?" Abby sniffled back her tears. "Is it Osiris, or Ptah, or Horus, or Amun-Ra?"

"None of these is the Creator."

Abby's forehead wrinkled as the term dredged up an old memory. "My ancestors believed there was only one god and that he made the heavens and the earth."

"Your ancestors were right," Jewel said. "Would you like to know more about Him?"

Stonecutter's Secret

ABBY got up the next day feeling better than she had in a long time. Sharing her pain with Jewel had lifted the secret burden from her soul. After a breakfast of goose eggs and pork sausage, which she devoured like a field hand, she led the Travelers toward Karnak Temple. They left Jeeter, Cyan, and their daypacks at the house, carrying what they needed under their tunics. As usual, the Baron had the most peculiar assortment of stuff.

Matterhorn teased his friend about his bulging pockets.

"Be prepared for everything . . ." the Baron said.

". . . and you'll be prepared for anything," Matterhorn finished. "I know, I know. I wrote it down, remember?"

The scorching sun had already ironed the day to a sharp crease by the time they reached Karnak. The Egyptians called it the "Most Select of Places." Matterhorn realized why when he saw the sixty-acre compound of buildings at the center of a 250-acre tract of trees and shrubs.

Near the entrance, a dozen golden-headed obelisks jabbed into the air to catch Ra's attention. Squadrons of Nile geese practiced touch-and-go landings on the sacred lake. To their left, the botanical garden of Thutmose III teemed with exotic animals and flora brought from lands as far away as Syria.

Behind a great wall of sandblasted stone loomed the main building—ten times larger than St. Peter's Cathedral in Rome would one day be. A colonnade of immense pillars connected the temple to a large courtyard, at the end of which sat the inner sanctums of Amun-Ra, Patron of the Pharaohs, and his wife, Mut.

Getting into the grounds presented no problem. People came from all over Egypt to pay homage to the gods. Abby explained the general layout of the place as they walked along a gravel path. "The open courts are for public festivals," she said, pointing to the right. "No one's allowed in the sanctuary except the priests."

Matterhorn saw the armed guards at the entrance and noted the wide berth everyone gave them.

"If the priest of Amun-Ra is inside," Kyl said, "we have to get in somehow. I am curious to know why he wants us dead."

Abby was eager to prove her usefulness. "There's a stone grotto on the far side that conceals a secret entrance. I'll show you." She led them around a line of shade trees to the east of the temple.

Matterhorn spotted an elaborate sundial as they passed a small courtyard. It brought to mind the Baron's boast of always knowing what time it was without the benefit of clock or watch. Matterhorn decided to test this claim. Blocking the Baron's view of the dial with his body, he asked, "What time is it?"

Aaron glanced skyward and answered without hesitation, "Nine-twenty."

Matterhorn darted into the courtyard to confirm the guess.

The Baron was right on the mark. How did he do that?

When they reached the grotto, they found it occupied by a group of pilgrims. Abby struck up a conversation and encouraged the party to visit the main courtyard where they could find a priest to present their offering to the gods.

"The cattle of Ra," Abby muttered after the pilgrims left.

"That's not very nice," Jewel said.

"It's what the Egyptians call themselves."

"And is that how you see yourself?"

"I'm part Habiru," Abby replied.

"One of the immigrants?" Kyl asked.

"My great-great-grandmother was."

Matterhorn sat on a limestone bench carved in the shape of a hippo with a flat back. He leaned against the wall and said, "This place is cool, but it seems to be missing something."

"Like a door," the Baron noted.

"Allow me," Abby said with a grin. She put her hands on two engraved circles to the right of the hippo's head and pushed. A three-foot section of wall swung inward, revealing a narrow stairway cut into the foundation.

Jewel shuddered involuntarily. "Here we go again." She followed Abby down a steep but mercifully short stairway. Elok waited till everyone reached the bottom before pushing the door closed and plunging them into pitch-blackness.

"Where are we?" Matterhorn asked. He resisted the urge to brighten this underworld with his Sword in Abby's presence.

"There's a maze of secret passages all through the complex," Abby said. "My uncle told me how the builders originally used them to move about without disturbing the priests. Workers could also rest down here without getting caught."

"Who else knows about these passages?" Elok asked.

"Only the stoneworkers. And they take a solemn oath not to reveal them under penalty of death."

"So why are you telling us?"

Abby smiled. "I'm not a stoneworker. I've never taken the oath."

"Lead on," Kyl said.

Abby lined everyone up, with each person putting a hand on the shoulder in front of him or her. She led the way into the musty gloom. Rock chips crunched under their sandals. Matterhorn could feel the tremor in Jewel's body. He gently squeezed her shoulder to let her know everything would be all right.

After several blind turns they climbed another stairway and surfaced inside the walls of the temple proper. The oppressive heat in the narrow passage made Matterhorn feel like a piece of white bread in a brick toaster. His two million sweat glands kicked into high gear. Slivers of light came from slits cleverly hidden in the cracks between the stones. Matterhorn stopped and pressed his face into a dusty cut. He put his finger under his nose to keep from sneezing. Through the vertical dash he saw a forbidden world of brilliant colors.

The center of the roof lay open to the sun, which illuminated stunning murals of gods and mortals on every flat surface. The supporting pillars were tattooed with hieroglyphics as high up as he could see. A few white-robed priests pattered about, their bald heads bobbing in time with their mumbled chants.

Abby pulled her human train farther into the sanctuary until they were crammed sideways into a slim corridor about thirty feet long and eighteen inches wide. She motioned everyone to find a peephole as angry voices rumbled on the other side of the wall.

Spy Hard

THE interior chamber had no windows. Oil lamps cast a surreal glow streaked with wisps of incense from lotus-shaped censers. Wall paintings as exquisite as anything in the palace graced the spaces between burnished columns. Full-winged vultures flew across the domed ceiling. Fat pillows slouched on a sleek divan pushed against the far wall. A polished teak desk occupied the center of the stately room.

Two men in animated conversation stood with their backs to the wall. After a heated outburst, the taller man in a yellow tunic swept a scroll off the desk with an angry backhand. The older man dropped to his knees and snatched the fine linen roll off the carpet. He had moved quickly for someone so elderly.

The *Book of the Dead* also known as the *Formula for Going Forth by Day*, contained incantations and spells to help departed souls pass safely through the underworld. The manuscript was central to the priest's craft and he handled it with reverence. Carefully returning it to the desk he snarled, "This scroll has been in Karnak for generations. Your behavior is intolerable."

"What is intolerable," the younger man snapped, "is your incompetence!"

"Then finish the job yourself," the old man hissed.

The man in yellow raised an arm as if to strike. Then, thinking better of it, he extended a helping hand. "We must not quarrel you and me. We are so close to accomplishing what we set out to do."

"Don't worry," the old priest said. "I will see to the foreigners. But why do they trouble you? It is only a merchant and a few servants."

"The sword described by the commander yesterday is not found in the company of ordinary men."

Matterhorn felt a stab of guilt at these words.

"Nor do commoners make fools of six assassins and then disappear. Do not underestimate them again. I warn you." The man in yellow brushed past the now pale priest and headed for the room's only door. Pausing to grab a large bronze censer, he squeezed its thick petals closed with his hands as if crushing a flower, smothering the flame within. His fingernails glowed red with the pressure, but no hint of effort or grimace of pain touched his face.

"I must leave soon and I do not want more trouble," he said. "See that I have none and you will have a long life. Fail me again and there will not be enough left of you for Anubis to weigh." He dropped the smoldering nugget and walked out.

The shock waves set off by this superhuman feat swept over the old man and into the wall. Abby's jaw went slack. Kyl showed no emotion while Elok's gaze remained fixed on the still swaying door curtain.

The Baron turned to Matterhorn and whispered, "Wow!"

Matterhorn figured the man must be a wraith.

Finally, the elderly Egyptian stirred. His spidery hands smoothed the wrinkles from the tunic that hung loosely on his gaunt frame. As he began to dress in his work clothes, he was transformed from a frail figure into an imposing official. First, he selected a purple vestment from a tall wardrobe. Next, he donned a large falcon pendant of *Ra-Harakhti*. Then he hid the age spots on his shiny scalp under an ornate headdress. Finally, he checked his appearance in the reflective metal. His thin lips crawled into a crooked smile. Satisfied, he strutted from the room like a rooster.

Matterhorn thumbed the sweat from his eyebrows and leaned toward Abby. "Who's that old geezer?"

"I don't know what a geezer is," she replied, "but that was Sebek, the high priest of Amun-Ra. He's named after the crocodile god, for he is said to devour his enemies."

"The high priest is nothing compared to the other man," Kyl said. "He is from my homeland."

"How did he crush that censer with his bare hands?" Abby wanted to know.

Instead of answering, Kyl said, "Is there a way to follow him and Sebek without being seen?"

Abby frowned and brushed a wisp of hair from her sticky forehead. "There are no secret passages that way. We would have to walk in the open, and that could be fatal. Only priests are allowed."

"We will protect you," Kyl said.

She stared up at him and asked, "Are you sure you want to do this?"

"With or without you," Kyl said.

Abby sighed. "Why not."

They inched back the way they had come until Abby found a small door into a seldom-used storeroom. Matterhorn was grateful to be out of the stone sauna. He must have lost five pounds in the last thirty minutes. What he wouldn't give for a gallon of lemonade.

Abby peeked into the corridor. "I don't know this part of the temple."

"We will figure it out as we go," Elok said. He started down the hall and the others followed with their senses on full alert. Matterhorn's hand rested on the hilt of his Sword. The Baron cupped a throwing star in his right palm. Between them, Jewel and Abby tiptoed like cats on caffeine.

At the first intersection Elok hesitated only a moment in the wide crossway before turning left.

Jewel stopped and said, "This way."

"The lady's right," agreed a nearby statue of Osiris.

Split Decision

THE Travelers froze as the statue's shadow came to life and stepped into the hall. Abby gasped at the unexpected transformation.

"Steady, mates," Nate said quietly. "This part of the temple's off limits to tourists. Guards find us here, we're cactus." Nodding in the direction Elok had chosen, he added, "That way leads to their barracks."

"Wh-who are you?" Abby stammered.

"This is Nate the Great," Jewel spoke up. "He's with us."

"What are you doing here?" Elok asked.

"Same thing you are."

"Did you see which way the high priest went?"

"Both men went straight," Jewel answered before Nate could.

"The Princess has a good conk," Nate said, touching his flat nose.

"I'll take that as a compliment," she replied. "The incense from the inner room is strongest straight ahead."

The Baron sniffed but smelled nothing. Matterhorn didn't even bother. He suspected Jewel had a better sense of smell than a bloodhound.

"Straight, then," Elok said.

At the next two intersections, Jewel directed them right and then left. They were now walking toward the late morning sun, which streamed into the hall from an open double doorway in the distance.

Matterhorn shielded his eyes with his left hand.

Jewel squinted and stepped into Elok's shadow.

As Abby slid in next to her, the girl's elbow brushed a vase. The fragile jar toppled off its pedestal and exploded on contact with the stone floor. Even before the accidental echo died away, they heard a commotion behind them.

"Sorry!" Abby squealed. "I couldn't see."

"Sounds like the cleanup crew's on the way," Matterhorn said. "We'd better find an exit."

They bolted through the open door toward which they had been heading and wound up in an interior courtyard. The surrounding buildings boxed in a private park filled with manicured flowerbeds and miniature trees. Under a tall arbor in each wall was an arched doorway like the one they had just come through.

"Now where?" Matterhorn cried.

"We will be harder to catch if we split up," Kyl said. "Nate, Jewel, and I will try to find the priest. Elok, take the others and get Abby out of here."

Elok looked at Abby, then at Kyl. Tension creased his face. He didn't want to leave his master, nor could he disobey a direct order. Matterhorn knew instantly how to resolve the dilemma. "The Baron and I will take care of Abby," he announced. "Meet us at her house when you can."

Kyl started to argue but Matterhorn grabbed Abby's arm and steered her toward the archway on the right. The Baron caught up and a moment later the trio was running through a petrified forest of red granite columns.

They heard yelling in the courtyard. Suddenly the door behind them crashed open. The rapid clip-clop of leather soles meant the race was on. If they lost, they died.

"Just like old times!" the Baron cried.

"I don't remember being chased by soldiers before!" Matterhorn panted.

Abby strained to keep pace with her long-legged companions. When they reached a wide flight of stairs, the Baron stopped and pulled a pint bag of clear liquid from under his tunic.

"Not the best time for a drink!" Matterhorn exclaimed from the fourth step.

Abby kept going, taking three steps at a bound.

The Baron put the baggie on the floor and jumped on it with both feet. The zip lock burst open and the clear fluid swooshed outward in a glistening slick. It made the hall look freshly waxed.

The first soldier to reach the wetness went down like a grandma on ice. So did the second.

"What is that stuff?" Matterhorn asked Aaron as they hurried after Abby.

"Micro-silicon antifriction beads. You couldn't cross that floor now in golf cleats."

"Another one of your creations?"

"Naturally." The Baron paused at the top of the stairs to take a deep bow. As he did, a spear whizzed over his bent form and splintered against the wall. Matterhorn drew his Sword just in time to decapitate a second deadly shaft.

More metal-tipped lumber was on the way when Abby shouted, "In here! There's a window!"

Keeping low, they scurried into what appeared to be a changing room for the priests. Linen ephods lay in neat piles on a low table. Colorful vestments with gold embroidery hung on a row of hooks. A full-length copper mirror split one wall. Sandals lounged in pairs beneath shelves of wigs on either side of the polished metal.

Matterhorn took all this in while racing to the window. Blue sky and freedom beckoned through the high stone arch. In three heartbeats he sat perched on the sill like a falcon ready for flight.

But what he saw fifteen feet below froze him into a gargoyle.

The height made Matterhorn uneasy, but what stopped him cold was the nearby knot of temple guards. The alarm had been sounded and already the crowds were being hustled toward the gates. How had so many soldiers been mobilized so quickly? Matterhorn wondered. Even with the Sword, he doubted they could fight their way to freedom. The last thing he wanted was to wind up in a kill-or-be-killed situation.

The Baron and Abby crowded into the window and nearly toppled Matterhorn. The prospect of almost falling sent shards of electricity around and around his rib cage. He fell back into the room and cringed against the wall. New sweat broke out on top of old.

Time was running out. Matterhorn knew the soldiers would circle around and come after them from the other end of the hall. He pulled at the hair behind his left ear, a nervous habit that helped him think. As he tugged, he got the strands of an idea.

He jumped to his feet and cried, "That's it!"

Sacred Sham

Chapter 23

WHAT'S it?" the Baron demanded.

"Hair!" Matterhorn almost shouted as he ran to the shelves and began trying on wigs. He grabbed an ugly yellow number that looked like roadkill and threw it at the Baron. Paraphrasing Sherlock Holmes he said, "You see, my dear Aaron, but you do not observe."

The Baron caught the hairpiece, made a sour face, and threw it back. "What are you babbling about? And don't call me dear!"

"Disguises," Matterhorn said. "Welcome to the priesthood. Get dressed!"

The Baron joined Matterhorn at the wig wall and selected a long, auburn number. "This must have been a horse's tail at one time," he said as he looked in the mirror.

"So what does that make you?" Matterhorn asked as he tucked his ponytail under a silver toupee.

"The butt of your jokes," the Baron retorted. He pulled a leopard-skin robe around his shoulders and admired the effect in the mirror.

"Don't wear that," Abby warned. "It's for the feast of Opet. You'll stand out like a cat in the royal kennels." She threw him a crimson robe and wrapped herself in a dark blue cloak with white piping down the sleeves.

The Baron put on the garment. Then he took an apple and a pomegranate from a bowl of wooden fruit on a corner table and stuffed them into his pockets.

"If you're going to steal," Abby said, "take something valuable."

The Baron ignored this and began helping Matterhorn knot several tunics together. When the makeshift linen ladder was complete, Matterhorn tied one end to a wall hook. He peered cautiously over the sill. Seeing the guards were gone, he tossed out the laundry. "You first," he told the Baron.

"Why me?"

"Because I'm not sure the hook will hold."

"That's what I like about you," the Baron said as he started out the window. "You're honest."

Abby went next, followed by Matterhorn.

"We can't go through the gates," the Baron observed as they crouched behind a flowering shrub. "These outfits won't fool anyone up close."

Matterhorn pointed and said, "But they should get us to the garden on this side of the lake. We might be able to get over the wall from there."

The Baron was skeptical. "It's still twenty feet high. We don't have Nate's Sandals you know."

"There might be ladders in that supply shed," Abby said, nodding toward a mud brick hut with slanted thatch roof near the wall. "The artists need some way to reach the paintings that are higher up."

That made sense to Matterhorn as he scanned the elaborate murals stretching to the top of the surrounding wall. "Let's check it out," he said.

Pretending to be deep in holy conversation, they had no trouble getting to the shed. But getting in was another matter. Matterhorn rattled the door and complained, "It's locked."

"Fascinating," the Baron said as he stooped to study the wooden device. Several pegs of differing lengths were fitted into holes in a sturdy bolt that held the door in place. A narrow slot in the housing was designed for a key with a matching set of pegs. When turned, the key would line up the internal pegs with the top of the bolt so the door could be opened.

The Baron began patting his pockets. "I need something long and slender to pick the lock."

"I have just the item," Matterhorn announced. He hiked up his priestly garments and smashed his size thirteen foot into the ingenious lock, reducing it to splinters.

"That'll do," the Baron said.

The shed contained good news—a ladder, and bad news—it was only ten feet long! That was barely half the length they needed. Matterhorn and the Baron argued about looking for another ladder until Abby, who was standing by the door, cried, "Soldiers!"

The sound of Matterhorn's footwork had attracted attention.

"Half a ladder's better than none," the Baron said. He grabbed the flimsy thing and sprinted out the door like a firefighter. Reaching the wall, he positioned the ladder and motioned Matterhorn up. "You first this time!"

The soldiers caught sight of the fugitives and picked up their speed, shouting for reinforcements as they ran.

"Climb!" the Baron yelled as he pulled the wooden pomegranate from his pocket.

As Matterhorn scurried upward, he heard the Baron's pitch thud into the chest of the closest guard.

"Hurry!" the Baron screamed, reaching for the apple.

Matterhorn stopped on the second highest rung. He spread his arms and dug his fingernails into the abrasive surface. "Climb up my back," he told Abby, who was right below him. She did so and knelt on his broad shoulders. Carefully she drew her feet under her and then stood. She reached for the top of the wall and pulled herself up.

Down below, the Baron had KO'd a second soldier with a wicked curve ball, er, apple. The guards did not retaliate with spears. Sebek wanted these intruders taken alive.

The Baron hustled up and over Matterhorn, who locked his knees and clawed the stones to keep from buckling under the load. Aaron made it topside just as the first soldier reached the ladder and kicked it away from the wall. He waited with drawn sword for Matterhorn's crash landing.

But Matterhorn was spared this pointed encounter when the Baron and Abby grabbed his outstretched arms. They pulled him up and in a flash the three were sprinting along the wide path atop the wall. When they came to a palm tree growing on the outside, Abby threw herself at it. She encircled the rough trunk with her arms and legs and shinnied to safety.

"Monkey see, monkey do," the Baron said as he jumped. Then it was Matterhorn's turn to leap and cling and slide painfully to earth.

By the time the temple guards made it through the gate and around to the tree, the escapees had shed their disguises and evaporated like manna at noon.

Subway to Safety

KYL, Elok, Nate, and Jewel had a somewhat easier time getting out of Karnak. They left the interior courtyard through the arch straight ahead. That's where the scent of the priest lingered. But first, Elok dashed across the garden and opened the door on the left a crack, hoping to misdirect the guards.

Nate took the point. He could smell the musky incense as easily as Jewel. In spite of their haste, they never caught sight of the cleric. By the time they heard the guards behind them, they had reached the far end of the corridor. Two sentries could be seen outside, spears at the ready.

Elok whispered something in Jewel's ear.

She smiled and said, "Of course." A moment later she walked boldly between the surprised sentries. "What's the matter, boys?" she purred. "Never seen a lady before?" They jumped forward and roughly grabbed her arms. Elok and Kyl slipped up behind the men and applied sleeper holds.

Nate helped Kyl drag the unconscious guards into the bushes while Elok closed the doors and pushed a ram-headed sphinx against them. The polished stone statue weighed a ton, but he handled it as if it had been carved out of soap.

The Travelers melted into the crowd. When they saw more soldiers moving among the people, Kyl said, "The search is widening. We cannot hazard the main gates."

"Don't have to," Nate said. He looked Kyl and Elok over and announced, "Tight, but you'll make it." He led them on a hedged path toward a sprawl of smaller shrines. "What's one thing that goes everywhere without being noticed?" he riddled his companions.

"Air?" Jewel guessed.

Nate remained silent.

"Water," Elok said.

Nate smiled. "Following water is often the best way to get in and out of places."

They left the path and went down a gentle slope to a grove of fig trees. A shaft had been dug at the bottom of this shallow basin as part of the drainage system. Nate removed the palmwood grate. "It's six meters to the canal that feeds the sacred lake. Brace yourself and scoot down."

He dropped into the hole and led by example. He didn't need his Sandals for this feat; it was simple pressure dynamics.

Jewel wiggled in after him. She squeezed her eyes shut and bit the insides of her cheeks. She told herself she could handle the short distance. Still, for someone with claustrophobia, six meters can be an eternity long.

Nate encouraged her from below and caught her when she dropped into the tunnel.

"It's so dark down here," she said with a shiver.

"Let there be light," Nate replied. His eyes had adjusted to the gloom and he spotted an old lamp hanging from a timber support. He lit the cloth wick with a small blue lighter.

"I didn't know bushmen carried lighters," Jewel said.

Nate grinned. "Beats whacking a flint."

The lamp produced more smoke than light and Jewel squinted against the sting. Nate took his knife and scraped some powder from a white patch on the wall, which he mixed with the lamp oil. The smoke disappeared.

"What did you put in there?"

"Salt," Nate replied, licking his fingers. "Leeches out of the limestone in this dampness."

Overhead, Kyl inched slowly downward. His shoulders barely fit inside the earthen tube. Elok had to pull his elbows into his stomach and hold his breath to get into the drain. Eventually the four stood in an eerie circle of light beside a half-filled channel.

"This path is for donkeys," Nate explained as they walked west.

"Donkeys?" Jewel asked. All she sensed were a couple of scorpions skittering at the edge of her animal radar.

"To dredge the canal," Nate replied. "This tunnel reaches to the Nile. Beaut job of engineering." He held the lamp higher so they could see how the subterranean conduit had been clawed out of rock and reinforced with rough beams. No pictures or hieroglyphics graced this manmade cave.

"Is this how you got into the temple grounds?" Elok asked.

"Once."

"How often have you been?"

"A few times."

"Did you notice a tall foreigner in a yellow tunic?" Kyl asked. "He had dealings with the high priest."

Nate nodded. "The bloke's been busier than a centipede in a shoe store the last few days. He's from up north in Giza."

"He is from farther away than that. He is from First Realm."

"What's he doing in Giza?" Jewel wondered.

"Stockpiling gold under one of the pyramids," Nate revealed. "Some of which he got from the high priest for murdering Tut."

"Sebek ordered Tut's execution?" Kyl asked.

Nate stopped the group to let a sand viper slither out of their way. "With Tut dead, the priest can put his own man on the throne."

"How did a stranger get near enough to the pharaoh to kill him?" Elok wanted to know.

"Inside help."

"From whom?"

Holding up two fingers, Nate said, "Heard two names, Horemheb and Aye. One's a general, the other an advisor."

"We met Aye at the palace while you were off sight-seeing," Jewel said. "Not the kind of man you'd want for a next-door neighbor. The Baron checked him out on the Net and learned he'll be the next pharaoh."

"Case closed," Nate said.

"Not quite," Elok replied. "Horemheb has a power-hungry reputation. The guards in the Valley speak openly of his ambitions. He would not be above making a move for the throne."

"Whoever it is isn't done," Nate added grimly. "Queen's next."

Famous Footwear

JEWEL had been about to ask if they could rest for a minute, but Nate's revelation brought a new urgency to their escape. The sooner they got above ground the better. Quickening her pace, she said what everyone was thinking. "We've got to warn the Queen."

"Getting back into the palace will be difficult after that business with the commander," Elok said. He briefly told Nate what had happened.

"Security's not so tight at the Queen's residence," Nate offered. "Talk to her there."

"You know where it is?" Elok asked.

Nate nodded.

Jewel was amazed. "How did you find out so much in such a short time?"

Nate did a small jig that made the emeralds in his Sandals glitter. "Helps to have the right shoes."

Elok smiled. "Are you aware the Maker created those Sandals for the Captain of the Praetorians?"

Nate was.

Knowing each of the Ten Talis reflected some aspect of the Maker's character, Jewel asked, "What do they represent?"

"Have you not read the inscription?" Elok asked.

Nate stopped and lowered the lamp.

Jewel read the script on the golden strap: *Stand firm in Me and you will never fall.*

"So," she said, "they symbolize stability."

"And steadfastness," Elok added. "Also firmness and constancy. Whoever wears the Sandals will never be off balance."

They started walking again and Jewel asked, "Why would the Captain give them up?"

"For the same reason many of the Talis were secreted out of the Realm," Kyl said, taking over the explanation. "To keep them from falling into heretic hands."

"I'm still not clear why the heretics want them," Jewel said.

"Because carrying a Talis makes one immune to the negative effects of time travel," Kyl said. "Since they are eternal, without beginning or end—"

"Wait a minute," Jewel interrupted. "I thought the Maker created the Talis."

"He fashioned them *before* time," Kyl said, "not *in* time. That makes them eternal, which means they are unaffected by time travel. So is any person who carries one."

Jewel understood now. "The heretics don't want the Talis for what they represent—"

"But for their traveling immunity," Kyl finished.

"Which they'll use to change history like they're doing here in Thebes," Jewel said, brushing a spider web out of the way. "But why mess with Earth at all? I thought First Realm didn't interfere with other worlds."

"The doctrine of noninterference has always been our creed," Kyl said. "Only when a civilization shows itself stable and mature do we make contact. But in the case of Earth, some on the Prima Curia are concerned that humans will destroy themselves and ruin the only mirror world of First Realm yet discovered. They want to secretly intervene and steer your future away from the nuclear abyss."

"What is the Prima Curia?" Jewel interrupted.

"Ruling council of the Realm," Kyl said. "They have not approved the scheme, but a few heretics are taking matters into their own hands."

"Praetorians trying to stop them?" Nate asked.

"Certainly," Kyl said. "But even Praetorians do not time-travel without protection."

"Since I have the Sandals, how's the new Praetorian Captain getting around?"

"They have no captain now," Elok said. "The last one never returned from hiding the Talis. He is the one who gave you the Sandals."

"Why me? Why not another Praetorian?"

"Because there are traitors in the Propylon," Elok went on. "Queen Bea must suspect this, for she could have taken them from you and selected a new captain."

Condensation dripped on them like slow rain as they talked and walked through the dank stillness.

The mention of Bea caused Jewel to ask, "Did the Queen send you to Egypt?"

"No." Kyl chose his next words carefully. "The heretics know all that goes on in the palace and the Propylon. They would soon find out what the Queen knows. Our presence here is a secret and must remain so. You cannot tell anyone. Do you understand?"

It would be hard to keep a secret from the Queen, but Jewel finally nodded agreement. After a few moments, so did Nate.

A glowing pinpoint in the distance slowly dilated into blue sky above brown water. Before they reached the exit cut into a small bluff, Nate handed the lamp to Jewel and jumped into the canal. "I'll make sure the coast is clear," he said before submerging.

A short time later, the top of his bristly head appeared twenty yards offshore.

"Oh no," Jewel gasped. Her mouth went suddenly dry as she sensed an enormous creature swimming toward Nate. "Watch out!" she screamed as she ran from the tunnel.

Nate had spotted the eyes and snout before he had heard Jewel's warning. The Nile croc was larger than the ones back home. His sixteen-foot body and sixty-six sharp teeth put him at the top of the food chain.

Nate's only defense was to become invisible, a skill he had worked hard to master. Through long practice he had developed the ability to go ectothermic: to lower his body temperature several degrees. He could slow his metabolism and heart rate as well. If he didn't move or give off heat, most predators couldn't find him. He took a deep breath and went log-rigid.

The big reptile glanced warily at the three noisy humans on the riverbank and decided to find a quieter place for a nap. As he glided to deeper water, he came close enough to bump the piece of human driftwood with his tail.

Nate rolled with the blow, his arms and legs as stiff as dead branches.

The croc stopped at the contact.

So did Jewel's heart.

Elok grabbed a rock and walked into the water. His pitch thudded off the animal's back. The croc turned slowly toward shore.

Easy there, big boy, Jewel mentally told the beast. We're not worth your bother.

With a powerful swish of its tail the crocodile headed downstream.

Nate waited another minute before cautiously propelling himself to land with slight swirls of his feet.

"That was close," Jewel said with a sigh of relief.

Wiping the water from his face, Nate replied, "No worries. The croc wasn't hungry or we might've had a go."

Kyl smiled at this lack of fear. "Who would have won?"

"I've wrestled crocs on land," Nate said without boasting. "Trick is to get on top and cover their eyes. Confuses 'em. But not a creature alive can take a croc in the water. If he's hungry, you're lunch."

Parting Ways

IT didn't take long for the 100-degree heat to raise Nate's body temperature to normal as the group hurried to Bahari's. When they reached the house sometime later, Jeeter ran circles around Kyl's legs until being scooped up in a playful embrace. Cyan rested in the shade of the garden wall and meowed for Jewel's attention. The two animals were different as night and day and couldn't stand each other.

Elok was about to head back to Karnak when a cheery "Yell-O" made it unnecessary. Matterhorn, the Baron, and Abby trooped onto the porch and everyone began talking at once. Kyl signaled for silence. "You can all take turns when we are inside."

Abby sent a servant to ask her father to bring some perch home for supper. She made her guests comfortable in a large sitting room where each group told the other of their escape from the temple precinct. When Matterhorn came to the part about sliding down the palm tree, he held up his scraped forearms. "Abby not only runs like a gazelle, she climbs like a monkey. A guy can get hurt trying to keep up with her."

The most interesting information was Nate's news about the deal between the high priest and the man from Giza. "The priest said something about being ready when the seventy days were up."

"Tutankhamen is still pharaoh while his body is being embalmed," Abby offered by way of explanation. "That takes seventy days. Only after he's sealed in his tomb can a new king be crowned."

Elok asked if she had any idea how the next pharaoh would be chosen.

Abby beamed with self-importance at knowing the answer. "Because Pharaoh had no son, whoever marries his widow will become king."

"And what if *she* dies before marrying?" Jewel asked.

Abby wasn't sure, but she took a guess. "A successor would be chosen from the royal court."

If true, this confirmed what the Travelers already knew: the Queen was in peril. Kyl sent Elok to buy a boat so they could get back and forth from the portal tomb in the Valley of the Kings. He didn't want to stay at Bahari's another night.

When Bahari came home with the fixings for supper, he tried to hide his uneasiness at seeing the strangers again. He relaxed when Kyl said, "We have a place to stay on the West Bank. We will be leaving after dark."

Abby felt the same conflict as the night before when she had almost been stabbed in her sleep. Part of her wanted to go with Jewel and the others, part of her wanted to stay home where it was safe. Today she had come within a whisker of getting caught in the sanctuary at Karnak, which would have resulted in instant death.

In the end, she would have no say in the matter. Kyl would not take her and her father would not let her go.

In true Middle Eastern fashion, Bahari acted the gracious host, setting a lavish feast for his guests. Their presence made him edgy, but it also gave him the chance to indulge two of his favorite pastimes: showing off his wealth and shoving food into his mouth.

The banquet began with fresh salad, followed by babaganoush, a dish featuring mashed eggplant. Next came fish and basmati rice, laced with little green peppers hot enough to remind Matterhorn of jalapeños.

Elok got back in time to finish off the perch and rice. He reached for the Baron's discarded peppers and casually popped one into his mouth as if it were a cherry tomato.

Matterhorn was impressed. He took two peppers and ate them like after-dinner mints as a culinary challenge to the big man.

Elok scooped the rest of the Baron's peppers into his mouth and chewed contentedly. His bald head turned red and glistened with sweat. He dabbed his runny nose with a napkin.

Matterhorn was picking more peppers from the rice when Kyl put an end to the fiery duel. "Did you find a boat?" he asked Elok.

Elok nodded as he bit into a lump of white cheese to smother the fire. When he could feel his tongue again, he said, "I purchased a sixteen-foot skiff."

"Then we should cross the river without more delay," Kyl announced.

Amidst the hasty farewells, Jewel hugged Abby and said, "Can I ask a favor? Would you take care of Cyan until we come back?"

"I'd love to," Abby agreed.

"Can I ask the same for my friend?" Kyl said. "That is if I can find him."

"Jeeter's in the trees out back," Abby said. "And, yes, I'll watch him."

"I can take care of that animal for you," Bahari said with a wink. "Monkey is a rare delicacy. Fried with onions and leeks, it makes a—"

"He's joking," Abby said with a nervous laugh.

Kyl smiled at Abby. "If anyone can keep Jeeter safe, you can." To Bahari he said, "Your daughter is a resourceful girl."

"Takes after her mother," Bahari replied. "Come, I will walk with you to the river." The sooner these strangers were out of his house the better.

On the way to the dock, Jewel stopped at an outdoor market to replace her supplies of plants and herbs. With Kyl's money she bought fresh chamomile tea, which the locals called "Herb of the Sun." The imported valerian root was expensive but well worth the price. Ground into powder, it made a potent sedative. She even found willow bark, a natural painkiller that would one day be refined into aspirin. Her last purchase was a small bouquet of yellow flowers.

After a final flurry of good-byes, the Travelers shoved off.

Abby held Cyan with one hand and waved with the other. She wondered what business her new friends had among the dead on the far shore.

"Good riddance," Bahari muttered under his breath.

Date Night

THE evening calm left the square sail as limp as a deflated balloon, so Elok reached for one oar and Matterhorn took the other. Soon the graceful craft was tickling across the Nile's smooth belly. When Elok increased his speed, Matterhorn answered with a burst of his own. Each raised the tempo in turn as they continued their friendly competition from supper. When they neared the West Bank, Kyl had to order them to stop or they would have rowed the boat halfway up the Valley of the Kings.

They avoided the main docks and turned upstream to a thick stand of eucalyptus trees. Several red-billed ibis were fishing from the overhanging branches. The birds complained loudly and flew off when the Baron jumped from the boat to guide it through the tangle of roots. "You go ahead," he told the others when they reached solid ground. "I'll camouflage the skiff and catch up. I'd like some time to myself."

"We cannot leave you in the dark," Elok said. "You will never find the tomb."

"Once I've been to a place," the Baron said confidently, "I can find my way back. I have a knack for directions."

"All right," Kyl said. He had seen enough to know these Travelers could take care of themselves.

"I'll whistle when I'm inside so you'll know it's me," the Baron told Elok. "I've seen how you treat intruders."

"Be careful," Matterhorn said. He would have offered to stay behind, but he suspected his friend would have company soon enough.

Matterhorn was right, for after everyone left, the Baron got into the boat and paddled a short distance from shore. Then he took a small vial from his pocket and pulled the stopper. A mist rose into the night and glistened into the shape of a beautiful woman.

"Where are we?" Sara asked as she pirouetted like a ballerina. She had on the simple gray shift she wore before going shopping in a new place.

"Glad to see you, too," the Baron said. "This is Egypt in the time of the pharaohs. Matterhorn, Jewel, and I were brought here from America. The story is almost as long as the journey."

"Tell me everything!" Sara cried. "I love stories!" She sat down across from the Baron, their knees almost touching. Dropping her dainty chin into her hands she leaned forward. Her blue eyes never left his as he told her about Elok and Kyl and Abby and Karnak.

While he talked, a part of the Baron's mind flashed back to when he had first met this lovely creature above a millpond in Ireland. She had saved him and Matterhorn from a fiery death. She had also rescued him and Jewel from drowning—had it only been a few days ago?

He remembered with shame not wanting to take Sara along when Queen Bea ordered him to. And yet, tonight, he couldn't wait to see her and talk to her again.

And talk he did, for almost two hours.

Sara interrupted from time to time with questions about things she didn't understand. As a water nymph, she had never heard of a "desert" before. She couldn't imagine the blistering heat or baking dryness the Baron described. "How can that be?" she asked, splashing water on Aaron. "This river's so big. I cannot sense either end of it."

He splashed back with an oar and smiled. "That's because it's the longest river in the world. But it's also the only water in Egypt. Away from here you couldn't find enough H_2O to materialize."

"Does that mean you won't let me stay out?" Sara pouted.

"I'd love to, but we can't chance it."

"Will you talk to me when you are by the river?"

"Whenever I can. I promise."

"Just give me five minutes to look around," Sara begged.

"Take ten."

Sara disappeared in a giggle. The Baron rowed back to shore and pulled the boat into the trees. He covered it with fallen branches and by the time he finished, Sara had returned.

"What a wonderful river!" she exclaimed. "But I see what you mean about the country. I have never seen such barrenness. I could not survive out there."

"That's where I have to go tomorrow," the Baron said. "And that's why you have to stay in your vial."

"I brought you something," Sara said, ignoring the small tube in his hand. She took a finely worked gold chain from around her neck and handed it to him.

"Where'd you get this?"

"There's a small barge on the bottom not far from here. It's full of the stuff. I prefer gems myself, but I understand humans like gold."

"I can't keep this," the Baron protested.

"You don't want my gift?"

"It's not that. Travelers aren't supposed to take things from the places they visit."

Puzzled, Sara said, "Not even from the bottom of a river?"

"Well—"

"I only wanted to show my gratitude for all your kindness. I'm sorry if I broke the rules."

The Baron didn't know what to say, so he settled on "Thank you." He would figure out what to do with the necklace later. "Time for me to go."

"Remember your promise," Sara said as she shimmered into mist.

With a happy heart, the Baron put the vial away, along with the gold chain, and started toward the tomb.

Soon he had unexpected company. A pack of hyenas picked up his scent and circled closer to check him out. No way could he avoid these mangy scavengers. They had excellent night vision and were among the fastest animals on four feet.

He knew enough not to try. Instead he stopped and crouched down to present a more appealing target. From a pocket he pulled a flat aluminum casing the size of his thumb. This specially designed LED light put out a powerful beam that could be seen for miles.

Emboldened by the stillness of their prey, the animals moved in for the kill. When the leader got within ten feet, the Baron suddenly flashed him with the light. The blinded creature howled in surprise as Aaron swept the light across two more pairs of eyes.

The hyenas broke ranks and ran for the hills with the Baron's loud laugh rolling after them.

Return Policy

MATTERHORN heard the Baron whistling toward the storeroom in the bowels of the tomb. The light from the torch that Elok had left burning by the entrance soon filled the doorway. Matterhorn waved his partner over to the pile of rugs. Jewel came from behind a makeshift partition and said by way of greeting, "Let me see your arm."

The Baron added his torch to the three already burning in wall brackets and offered his forearm for inspection. Jewel removed the dressing she had applied earlier. "This cut is getting infected," she said as she pressed the swollen gash.

"Ouch!" the Baron cried. With all the activity of the past few hours, he hadn't noticed the pain. "I've got some antibiotics in my first-aid kit," he told Jewel.

"So do I," she replied. "And mine are fresher." As carefully as she could, she eased the jagged edges of skin apart and cleaned the wound with water. Then she sprinkled grains of brown sugar into the cut to dry the tissue and kill the bacteria. Finally, she applied white willow leaves and tightly bandaged the arm. "These will draw out the remaining inflammation," she explained. "By the way, how's Sara?"

"Was it that obvious?" he said as he plopped down next to Matterhorn, trying not to bump the latest in his long line of travel injuries.

"As mumps on a giraffe," Nate said. He sat cross-legged on a cushion cleaning his fingernails with a knife. Its red-and-black stone blade looked like a long narrow arrowhead with a bone handle.

"Sara's fine," the Baron said as he patted his pocket. "It's too dry for her anywhere but near the river. I don't know what would happen if her essence completely evaporated—and I don't want to find out."

Jewel still had a bit of doctoring to do and she motioned Matterhorn over. "You're next."

"What for?"

"First-degree sunburn," Jewel said. "This should help." Earlier, she'd made a salve of olive oil, honey, and calendula, the yellow flower from the market. Its soft petals were excellent for repairing damaged skin while the honey provided a natural antiseptic. She dabbed the sticky balm on Matterhorn's face, arms, and feet.

"Thanks," he said, trying not to wince.

"Where are Kyl and Elok?" the Baron wanted to know.

As if on cue, the two returned from a private conference down the hall. "Tomorrow we will divide into groups again," Kyl said. "Nate will take me and Jewel to the queen's palace. We have to warn her of the danger she faces. Elok, Matterhorn, and the Baron will track down the man from Giza. Get some rest; we leave early."

"Do you trust those two?" the Baron asked when they were alone again.

"I do," Jewel said. "They're not telling us everything about themselves, but they seem loyal to Queen Bea."

"We can ask about them next time we see Her Majesty," Matterhorn said.

"No we can't," Jewel replied. "Kyl made Nate and me swear not to say anything to the Queen."

"Why?" Matterhorn asked.

"He's afraid of spies."

"That's rather convenient," the Baron pointed out. "Kyl says he's a royal, but he forbids us to check his story." Nodding at Nate he added, "Maybe we should send the Invisible Man to eavesdrop this evening."

"No, we shouldn't," Nate said. "A bloke's a friend until he proves himself an enemy."

Matterhorn wanted to write that phrase down. He reached into his pack for his quote book and found something more pressing to do.

When he'd taken the medallion, Matterhorn didn't want anyone to know it. Now he didn't care who saw him return the stolen object. He took the gold piece from his gear and put it in the trunk where he'd found it; then turned to face the inevitable questions. He would admit his theft and tell how the light from the Sword of Truth had burned his heart, inside and out.

But the questions never came. Everyone watched, but no one needed an explanation. Jewel winked and waved good night before tucking behind the partition. Nate yawned and curled up in a ball. The Baron said, "Sweet dreams," and smothered the torches with a rag.

Matterhorn lay down and let out a deep, contented sigh. As he drifted toward sleep, he heard a familiar voice in his head.

"*You wanted a souvenir of your travels. I have given you one.*"

Matterhorn felt a tingling in his chest wound.

"*Whenever you travel, this scar will remind you that I have called you to serve others, not yourself. Serve well and you will serve long. Do not worry about your needs along the way. I will see to those. I give you the promise I give all My servants: Take care of My business and I will take care of yours.*"

Matterhorn started to thank the Maker for the scar and its lesson when the voice laughed. The delightful sound filled him with such joy that it seemed to levitate him several inches off the floor. He basked in the echo of that promise for a long time. Then he lit his Sword just enough to find his quote book. He wanted to record the Maker's promise while it was still vivid.

He pulled the stubby pencil from the book's spine and turned to what should have been a blank page. Already written there in the same flowing script as on his Talis were these words:

Take care of My business and I will take care of yours.

Royal Heritage

SUNRISE the next morning caught the Travelers trekking through the wrinkled khaki cliffs to the river. The Baron toyed with letting Sara out of her vial on the trip across the Nile, but the ride was too short and the day's business too urgent. He did secretly drop the gold chain she had given him into the water, recalling Matterhorn's actions from the night before. He would explain his reasons to Sara later.

Docking near the fish market, they separated, agreeing to meet at Bahari's shop by nightfall. "Can you get us to Karnak?" Elok asked, as he and Matterhorn followed the Baron into the city.

"I've been there once, haven't I?" Aaron answered.

Nate led Kyl and Jewel in the opposite direction, and in a surprisingly short time they came within sight of the Queen's residence. Nate had them hide in an empty building while he went to survey the palace grounds.

"If we make it to the Queen," Jewel asked while they waited, "how will you get her to take your warning seriously?"

"She knows her life is in danger," Kyl said, offering Jewel a slim hip flask. "She is afraid. I saw it in her eyes."

"That doesn't mean she'll trust you," Jewel replied after a swig of water. "You're a total stranger and an intimidating one at that. Maybe I should talk to her first."

Kyl thought this over. "Your age and gender might be less threatening. I see that you have gained the confidence of another Queen." Pointing to the onyx wolf hanging from Jewel's right ear he said, "When did Bea give that to you?"

"When she asked me to help find the hidden Talis," Jewel replied.

"Do you know how to use it?"

"Yes," Jewel said, and then decided to ask a few questions of her own. "You say you're one of the royals. What do you do in First Realm?"

"I am a Magistrate."

"A Magistrate?"

Although Realm information was shared with Travelers on a need-to-know basis, Kyl decided to expand Jewel's education. "The Maker chose a special family to rule the Realm," he told her. "From one couple and two sons, they have grown into a mighty dynasty. Now we serve in three capacities. The Praetorians are the Guardians of the

Propylon and the portals. The Prelectors see to the education of the young and the preservation of the sacred truths. The Magistrates handle legal and governmental tasks."

"Soldiers, teachers, and judges," Jewel summarized.

"Among other things," Kyl said. He checked outside and noted how deserted the area was compared to the crowds they had encountered at Pharaoh's palace. There was no sign of Nate.

Taking advantage of the extra time, Jewel pressed to learn more about her mysterious companion. She would have pegged him for a Praetorian, but she could also picture him as a Magistrate. He had an air of authority and the quiet confidence of someone used to issuing moral decrees and passing sentences.

"When did you decide to come to Earth?" she asked.

"After the heretics struck down the King," Kyl replied.

Jewel shivered at the controlled rage in his tone. "Why did they do it?" she asked.

"Because he learned of their scheme and decided to put the Talis they needed beyond reach," Kyl answered. "They tried to stop him but were too late."

"Why not go directly to the governments of Earth?" Jewel asked next. "Expose the heretics and what they're trying to do."

Kyl laughed softly. "If humans learn of First Realm, they will discover the portals, then the Propylon and time travel. As a race you are not ready for such knowledge."

The temperature in the mud brick enclosure was rising uncomfortably. Kyl wiped his sweaty brow with his forearm.

"So that's why you and Elok are working undercover?" Kyl nodded.

"Won't you be missed back home?"

"I have a capable replacement," Kyl said.

"I know you're worried about traitors among the royals," Jewel said, "but I could tell Queen Bea privately about you. It would encourage her to know what you're—"

"No!" Kyl said forcefully. "All things in good time."

Five minutes later, Nate reappeared with good news. "Queen's in her sitting room, second floor, west wing. Let's toss the Princess through the window and see if they hit it off." He had also come to the conclusion that Jewel would make a better first impression.

"What about palace security?" Kyl asked.

"Nothing we can't avoid," Nate said.

The Queen's palace occupied the northeastern corner of a walled complex the size of two football fields. Sneaking through a servants' entrance in the east wall, the intruders darted around storage rooms and outbuildings. They skirted a large courtyard where children were noisily playing and crept alongside the central hall until they reached the west wing.

Nate and Kyl made a stirrup of interlocked fingers. As soon as Jewel gave them her right foot, they launched her skyward.

There was only one problem with the launch: altitude. Too much of it.

Jewel shot past the window before she could react. She fell back to earth like a spent rocket booster—into Kyl's strong arms.

"What a ride! Can I go again?"

Nate grinned. "Got another ticket?"

The second toss was on target. When her shoulders came level with the window, Jewel stretched for the sill. One hand slipped off the smooth stone but the other caught the inside edge—and held.

On the Waterfront

HALF a city away, Elok, Matterhorn, and the Baron were parked in the shade across from the priests' entrance to Karnak. Like undercover cops, they were hoping to catch sight of either the high priest or the man in the yellow tunic.

Neither appeared, but an hour into the stakeout, Matterhorn saw a face he recognized. The captain of the palace guard walked through the gate flanked by two Nubian soldiers. These dark-skinned mercenaries were Elok-sized brutes.

"I thought only priests could go in there," the Baron said when the men entered unchallenged. "Do you think the commander is in on the conspiracy?"

"He is probably just a messenger," Elok said.

It wasn't long before the commander and his escorts came back outside and headed north.

"Shall we follow them or stay put?" Matterhorn asked.

"Let's go," the Baron said. "A thin lead is better than none."

Elok agreed.

Instead of going to the palace, the captain stayed on the main avenue until it left Thebes. Beyond the city, the road narrowed as it sliced through orange and lemon orchards. Sunlight dappled the foreground of this pastoral scene while corduroy-like sands rolled in the background.

Soon the citrus trees gave way to barley fields. Peasants worked their long-poled *shadoofs*, balancing weighted buckets to fetch water from the canals. The open countryside forced the stalkers to lag farther behind their quarry to avoid being seen.

Four miles from town they came to a grand estate built on a kink of the Nile. The three-story villa, fashioned of serene pink quartz, glittered above the ten-foot walls like a fantasy castle. Dreadlocks of greenery laced with pink flowers hung from roof gardens. Shady walkways of crushed rock snaked around large reception halls, parade grounds, and slaves' quarters. Blue lunch smoke haloed the open-air kitchen. Roses bloomed everywhere in mini-explosions of red and pink and tangerine.

Two wooden docks stretched out from the landscaped waterfront. Several sailboats clustered around one dock, while a massive barge occupied the other. Bare-chested workmen swarmed over the flatboat from stem to stern.

All these details could be clearly seen through the expansive open gates. The commander entered the estate while Matterhorn, the Baron, and Elok cut across a field and raced to the river. They backtracked toward the villa and crouched in the reeds.

"What now?" Matterhorn asked. "Wait for dark and try to sneak in?"

The Baron shook his head. "I don't want to spend the day in this heat." His skin had been baked pretzel-brown and coated with salt from evaporated sweat. Slapping his neck, he said, "These mosquitoes will eat us alive."

"We have no idea if this place has anything to do with the man from Giza," Elok pointed out.

"Then let's see if he's inside," Aaron said. Up came his tunic, *scritch* went a pocket tab, and out popped a pair of miniature binoculars. The spyglasses had a magnification factor of ten, yet fit in the palm of one hand. A silver film coated the top of the casing, which Matterhorn assumed was a solar collector. A stout wire poked an inch beyond the right side of the frame and ended in a small, perforated bud.

The Baron touched the tip of the wire and said, "This is a unidirectional mike. On a fully charged battery it can pick up sounds a mile away." He peered into the eyepieces and adjusted the focus knob. Static rattled out of a tiny side speaker. Because the barge appeared to be the center of activity, he began spying there.

By the time each of them had a long look, they knew all they needed to know. The barge was being loaded with gold bars and enough provisions for the 400-mile trip to Giza. It would leave tonight.

"What is happening at the pyramids may be the key to unraveling the heretic's plot," Elok said as he gave the binoculars to the Baron. "We must tell Kyl."

With that, he led the way out of the reeds and back through the barley to the road. Being in a hurry, they weren't as careful the second time they passed the pink palace.

Enjoying the view from a shaded balcony, the commander almost fell over the railing when he spotted the trio. The very men his new employer desperately wanted to find were just waltzing by his front door!

The soldier rushed downstairs with the news. As a reward for his alertness he hoped to be allowed to handle this matter personally. He had a score to settle with these foreigners, especially the one who had made a fool of him in front of his men. After a hasty word with the guard, he was allowed back into the sitting room where he had made his earlier report.

The man known as Carik stood at the window watching the dockworkers. He looked like a statue off his pedestal. His chiseled face had the cast of Aswan granite. The two-foot serpent coiled around his tanned forearm did not affect his calm manner. Saw-scaled vipers caused more deaths than any snake on earth, yet he wore one as a charm bracelet.

"Why have you returned?" Carik asked without taking his gaze from the waterfront.

"I saw the red-haired man with the sword," the commander blurted out. "He passed your front gates with his companions not five minutes ago. Give me the Nubians and I'll rid you of these troublemakers before sunset."

"Wait at the road for my men," Carik said as he stroked his poisonous pet. "They will know what to do."

After the soldier bolted from the room, Carik summoned his Nubian guards. "Go with the Egyptian. He will lead you to the Travelers. Take no action until you are sure you have found them all. There might be as many as five or six."

"And when we have them?" asked one of the ebony giants.

Carik cupped the serpent's head in his right hand. With a savage twist, he tore it off and tossed the writhing body at the Nubians. Blood spurted across the expensive carpet and splattered their feet. Neither man flinched.

"All threats to my plan must be dealt with accordingly," he said, throwing the head out the window. "No one can be allowed to interfere."

"No one."

Private Audience

MEANWHILE, back at the palace, things had gone well. The young Queen had been startled by Jewel's sudden appearance in her sitting room. More curious than frightened, she listened to the stranger's appeal for a private audience. "Invite them up," she commanded when she learned of Kyl and Nate waiting below. "But remember, my guards are right outside."

Jewel stuck her head out the window and gave a welcoming wave.

Nate made a stirrup with his hands. The much larger Kyl shot him a look that said, "Are you serious?"

The emeralds in Nate's Sandals twinkled a "no problem."

Kyl stepped up and was hoisted to the sill. Pulling himself inside, he turned to help Nate, but the bushman was already up.

The large room had murals of the goddess Bes stretching from the polished floor to a ceiling stenciled with pink rosette spirals. Deep-throated vases of fresh bouquets filled the space with fragrant aromas. Across from the window stood a slim statuette of Sekhmet with a golden sun disk on her head.

Queen Ankhesenamen sat at a vanity cluttered with alabaster vials and jars of ointments. Without all the makeup she wore in public, her round cheeks had the color and softness of apricots. Her eyebrows were plucked to perfection above feline green eyes.

The normally shy teen studied the men in the polished metal as she pulled an ivory-handled brush through her raven hair. "You are persistent," she said to Kyl.

Nate silently moved to the door to listen for unexpected company while Kyl stepped closer to Her Majesty. "And you are in peril," he said. "If you are as smart as I think, you know your husband did not die of natural causes."

"He was murdered," the Queen replied calmly, laying down the brush and facing her visitors. "My husband was betrayed by someone he trusted. I don't need a foreigner to tell me that."

"Whom do you suspect?" Kyl asked.

The monarch coyly folded her hands in her lap. "You are the prophet from afar. You tell me."

"Either the counselor Aye or General Horemheb," Kyl said.

The Queen's shoulders clicked back a few notches, thrusting her regal chin forward. "On what grounds do you accuse such high officials?" she challenged. "I have known Aye all my life. He was my husband's personal advisor and ruled Egypt in Pharaoh's name until a few years ago.

"And as for Horemheb, he's the Great Commander of the Army and Overseer of the King's Works. True, he comes from common stock, but he has served us well in Nubia, Libya, and Syria. He has even been given permission to construct a grand tomb at Saqqara."

The irony of the situation did not escape the Queen. She grimaced as she added, "My husband had not even started on his own House of Gold. We will have to make due with something in the Valley of the Kings."

"The assassin did not act alone," Kyl said. "The high priest and a stranger from Giza are also plotting to seize the throne. You will be their next target. You must leave at once."

Picking up her brush again, the Queen fussed with her hair. "I couldn't leave Thebes even if I wanted to. The funeral arrangements have barely begun."

"You don't have to flee, Your Majesty," Jewel said.

Kyl stared hard at Jewel. He did not like being contradicted.

Ignoring his cold blue glare, Jewel said to the Queen, "Summon Aye and Horemheb here under some pretense and I will unmask the traitor."

"And how will you do that?" the Queen asked skeptically.

"With this." Jewel took the Band of Justice from the belt beneath her tunic.

The Queen found herself gawking at the most beautiful gem she had ever seen—and that was saying a lot.

"Are you sure you know what you are doing?" Kyl asked Jewel.

She was not as much of a novice as he thought. Jewel had had some experience with the Talis among the Sasquatch. "With this I can see into the heart," she explained to the Queen. "All I need is to touch someone to read their deepest thoughts."

The Queen was used to the hocus pocus of the priests and astrologers, but she didn't put much store in it. She tilted her head sideways and thought about dismissing these odd strangers.

Reading this hesitation, Jewel quickly said, "I can demonstrate if you wish."

The Queen didn't protest, so Jewel slipped the Band on her head and rested her hand on the royal arm. Instantly a flood of emotions washed over Jewel through the mental connection. She plucked one poignant memory like a flower and bent to whisper into the Queen's ear.

The young monarch blanched whiter than her linen gown. She slumped in her chair and looked up into Jewel's open face. "H-how could you know that?" she stammered.

"The power is the Maker's, not mine," Jewel replied, touching the triangular ruby on her forehead. "With your help, we can use this to save your throne—and your life."

Trusted Traitor

WHEN the Queen regained her composure she said to Kyl, "I can believe what you say about Sebek having designs on the kingdom. I've never trusted that old croc. But the other two you mentioned have sworn oaths of allegiance to the throne. Both have risked their lives in Pharaoh's service. If one of them is a traitor, I must know it. Wait here while I speak to the captain of my guards."

After she left, Kyl said to Jewel, "Are you all right? The Talis can be a burden to use."

"This isn't my first time," Jewel said. "I'm getting the hang of controlling what I let in."

"Why did you not tell me what you had in mind?"

Jewel shrugged. "You would have tried to stop me."

"Perhaps."

"I got the idea from Queen Bea you know," Jewel added by way of explanation. "She hoped to use the Band to find her father's killers. If it would work in First Realm, why not in Egypt?"

The Queen of the Two Lands returned and reported on her hastily conceived plan. "I have sent for Aye and Horemheb as you requested. To get them here immediately I said that a plot on the throne involving the high priest has come to my attention. The traitor will come to discover how much I know. The innocent man won't ignore a possible threat to his position."

Sitting at her vanity once more, she said, "I have done my part; how will you do yours? Aye has seen you before. He may have you killed when he recognizes you."

"Give me slave's clothing, a wig, and some makeup," Jewel replied. "I'll disguise myself and wash the feet of your guests as hospitality requires. Kyl and Nate can hide in the closet."

This satisfied the Queen, who nodded at one of four curtained alcoves. Dresses of every design and fabric lined the sides while the back wall had six shelves of stylish wigs and royal headdresses. Scores of shoes littered the floor and made walking difficult.

"Careful," Jewel said as Nate and Kyl slipped inside. "There's a scorpion in the far right corner."

"How do you know that?" the Queen asked.

"I have this thing with animals," Jewel said.

"You can explain it to me while we fix your face," the Queen said. She rang for her lady-in-waiting and over the next thirty minutes they transformed Jewel into a homely servant. The heavy rouge and green eye shadow smothered her natural beauty as completely as the loose frock hid her youthful figure. She spun the Band of Justice backward so the stone was hidden under the jet-black wig and combed the coarse bangs over the white strip on her forehead.

The disguise was in place by the time a shuffling in the hall announced the arrival of Aye and Horemheb and a squad of soldiers. Leaving their bodyguards outside, the two officials stomped into the room.

The Queen sat at her vanity with Jewel brushing her hair. She fought to control her fear. These were powerful men, and one of them might be planning to kill her.

Jewel remembered the older man from the palace. He looked angry enough to chew rocks. But as grim as Aye appeared, his younger companion was even more upset. At five-feet-ten inches, General Horemheb was tall for an Egyptian. He had brooding eyes, heavy jowls, and jagged teeth due to the ever-present sand in desert cooking. His pleated leather kilt hung from a thick waist. Several of the fingers on his rough hands had been broken and poorly set.

Motioning the men to a low settee, the Queen said, "Please rest. Let my servant refresh you."

"We don't have time for this," the General scowled as he pinched the bridge of his nose. But he followed Aye's lead and sat down.

Jewel took the bowl and towel that had been placed by the door and began washing Horemheb's feet. She cleaned his skin and searched his soul while the Queen spun a conspiracy theory involving the high priest. Having been raised at court made her a skilled liar.

However, as seasoned veterans of palace intrigue, the men didn't buy her tall tale. They exchanged a sideways glance, then the General spoke with thinly veiled contempt for the impressionable teen. "Your Majesty should not listen to the babbling of fools. Sebek is an honorable man. Don't look for the hand of a mortal behind an act of the gods."

"The gods didn't kill my husband," the Queen retorted.

Aye raised a calming hand. "The untimely death was tragic," he said, "but we must look forward, not backward. You cannot afford to make as powerful an enemy as the high priest of Amun-Ra. Say nothing to anyone. If word reaches Sebek of your suspicions . . ." He left the dire warning unfinished.

Jewel removed Aye's leather sandals as he spoke. Washing his feet, she sifted his thoughts. Neither he nor Horemheb suspected the mental intrusion, such was the subtlety of the Band. For Jewel, it was like watching home movies, but not the kind she would have chosen.

These were greedy and ambitious men, driven by a ruthless lust for power. The General had been a man of war from his youth. The counselor had lived twice as long and had learned far more devious ways of imposing his will on others.

The Queen's voice interrupted Jewel's reflections. Her Majesty stood and nodded in acceptance of the rebuke. "These are difficult days," she said as if to justify her actions. "My husband is dead, and I don't know who will take his place, or what will happen to me."

"We will see that no harm comes to you," Aye promised.

"We will protect you with our lives," Horemheb added.

Both men sounded sincere, yet Jewel knew who was lying.

Final Crossing

BAHARI glanced up from his display table of fresh fish and saw the three heads like topsails on the horizon. He didn't have to see their faces to know that the tall foreigners had returned. His heart sank. But Abby's spirits soared when she recognized Matterhorn and the others. Could Jewel be far behind?

Abby leapt to her feet and threw her fillet knife at the post holding the back curtain. It stuck in the bull's-eye she had drawn there when she was ten. She hung her apron on the still quivering handle, pulled her tunic between her legs and hurdled the table.

All this commotion flustered Bahari. It was bad enough these foreigners kept coming to his stall. Why did Abby have to be so friendly to them? If they were up to no good, the authorities would think he was part of it.

"Where's Jewel?" Abby asked as she greeted the Travelers.

"On her way I hope," Matterhorn said. "Is there someplace cool we can wait for her and Nate and Kyl? I'm sweating like a pig at a luau."

The Baron laughed. "Sounds like something Nate would say."

"What's a luau?" Abby asked.

"Never mind," Matterhorn said.

Elok went to check on their boat while Abby took Matterhorn and the Baron under the pier where they could get the sun off their backs. She peppered them with questions they didn't want to answer. They were rescued when Bahari hollered at her to return to work.

Matterhorn slipped off his sandals and dug his heels into the damp sand. "Can I see those little binoculars again?"

"I call them spynoculars," the Baron said as he handed them over. "The tricky part was designing a mike with decent range that would filter out ambient sound."

Matterhorn scanned the far shoreline. "Do you use any of your gadgets at home?" he asked. "You could become the next Edison. Did you know he had over one thousand patents?"

"He received 1,093 patents to be exact," the Baron said, "including four that were issued after he died. Edison and I have a lot in common, including dyslexia."

"You have dyslexia?" Matterhorn said.

"Don't look so shocked. A lot of creative people have it. It just means I have a different style of learning. But to answer your question, no I don't use my inventions at home. I don't want to draw attention to myself because it might interfere with my traveling."

"Do you travel a lot?"

"As much as I can."

The intensity of the Baron's tone surprised Matterhorn. "Why? Is something the matter at home?"

Aaron let out a long breath. "Life can be a pain sometimes. I do okay in school, but not great. I don't like to read unless I'm really interested in the subject. I don't do well on tests either. I learn best by taking things apart and putting them back together." He picked up a handful of rocks and began skipping them across the water.

Matterhorn said nothing.

"My mom's great," the Baron continued after a while, "but she has two jobs and I hardly see her. I get home from school or baseball practice, fix my own supper, and fool around on the computer. We live in an apartment so I don't have a yard, a garage, or even a basement. That's why I set up my own place in the Propylon."

Matterhorn felt guilty for taking his basement lab and backyard tree house for granted. He also took for granted having two loving parents, as well as a brother and sister. He scooped up some rocks of his own and began throwing. "Does your father ever come around?"

"Never," the Baron snapped as he bounced a stone hard against a rotting pylon. "He left when I was three. I haven't heard a word since. I don't know if he's dead or alive."

"It must be tough not having a dad."

"My uncle Shaun does stuff with me. He's the one who taught me how to throw a baseball. That's one thing I do pretty well."

"Did he give you your nickname?"

The Baron shook his head. "I gave it to myself when I was seven. I used to daydream about being Aaron the Baron, avenger of wrongs and doer of noble deeds." He smiled at the childhood recollection. "The first time I met Queen Bea it seemed like a make-believe adventure, so I introduced myself as Aaron the Baron."

"What's your real name?"

"Aaron James."

Just then a delighted yelp rose out of the din above.

"Sounds like Abby," Matterhorn said.

"The Princess and company must be here," the Baron concluded.

They found Jewel, Nate, and Kyl in front of Bahari's place. Abby and Jewel jabbered away while the nervous fishmonger tried to hustle everyone out of sight of his nosy neighbors.

The flies in the back of the stall where they ended up were thicker than scales on a sunfish, but at least the place was semiprivate. They found crates or baskets to sit on and arranged themselves in a sloppy circle. Cyan left the catfish head she had been playing with in the corner and assumed her favorite position on Jewel's lap.

Matterhorn answered Kyl's question about the man in yellow by saying, "We found him at a villa upriver, but he's leaving tonight on a barge full of heavy metal, if you get my drift."

"That is not good," Kyl said.

"Indeed not," Elok said as he slipped silently through the curtains to join them. "I brought our skiff to the dock. We should depart for the West Bank at once." He didn't have to mention their need for privacy in order to plan their next move.

"Can I go with you this time?" Abby asked hopefully.

"No," Kyl replied as kindly as he could. "We may not return to Thebes."

"We're just passing through," Jewel added. "This is your home."

Abby kept the pout from her chin but couldn't stop the moisture in her eyes. She'd finally found a true friend, only to have her leave as mysteriously as she had come. Blinking back the tears, Abby removed a purple scarab ring and tried to give it to Jewel. "Promise to remember me whenever you look at this."

"I don't need a ring to remember you," Jewel said as they embraced.

"I'll remember you too," the Baron said, giving Abby a sideways squeeze. "Promise me I'll be the last of your marks."

Abby laughed and returned the hug. "I promise. No more thieving."

After thanking Bahari for his hospitality, the Travelers followed Elok to the boat and rowed away.

Abby and Bahari weren't the only ones watching the skiff glide westward.

The commander and the Nubians had stealthily tracked Matterhorn and the others to the fish market. They waited. They watched. And now they lost no time in stealing a boat and starting cautiously after their prey.

The Egyptian chuckled as his stoic companions drew quietly on the oars. He found it wickedly funny that the foreigners were heading for the City of the Dead.

This would make it so much easier to dispose of their bodies.

Speed Bump

A HUNDRED yards from shore, the Travelers began discussing the day's events. Nate and the Baron had the oars this trip. The latter added more details to Matterhorn's report. Then Jewel dropped her bombshell.

"General Horemheb killed Tut," she announced. "He snuck into Pharaoh's bedroom and smothered the King in his sleep. I saw the memory of the gruesome deed when I washed the General's feet. And that's not all. He plans to kill Aye and the Queen next. The army is behind him and the wealth of Amun-Ra is at his disposal. He's made some sort of pact with the high priest."

"Sebek's crooked as a roo's hind leg," Nate said.

"But we know Aye will be the next pharaoh," Matterhorn pointed out. "Unless that future has already been changed."

"Aye may yet be pharaoh," Kyl said, "if the Queen marries him quickly. That is what we advised Her Majesty to arrange before we left."

The Baron remembered seeing the two together in the

palace and winced. "He's old enough to be her grandfather. Why would she marry him?"

"Marrying Aye would make him the next pharaoh," Jewel reminded the Baron. "The Queen doesn't love him, but together they can deal with Horemheb. It's about the only chance she has."

"How does the man from Giza fit into all this?" Matterhorn asked.

"I'm not sure," Jewel replied. "My contact with the General was too short to learn everything I'd hoped."

The conversation went on until a gentle bump on the bow signaled an end to their crossing. As on the previous evening, the Baron stayed behind to hide the boat and visit with Sara.

Released from her vial, the nymph shot upward into the growing dusk and vanished. When she returned a few minutes later, her normally cheery face was tight with concern.

"There's a boat coming this way!" she blurted out. "Two men in it just threw a third fellow into the river!"

The Baron thought about the men he had tracked earlier in the day and asked, "Are they dark-skinned and huge?"

Sara's nod confirmed his fears.

He didn't have time to figure out why the soldiers had turned on the Egyptian officer; he had to warn the others. "Gotta go!" he cried as he raised the vial for Sara to enter.

"I can't leave that man to drown!" she protested.

"Those brutes broke his arm before throwing him over-board. He'll never make it to shore, especially when the crocodiles catch the scent of blood."

Sara was right. The Baron had little sympathy for the Egyptian, but he didn't want him dead. "Do what you can," he told her, "then meet me up the trail. I won't go far. Hurry!"

Sara disappeared and the Baron tucked his tunic into his belt and started for the tomb. He was grateful for the cool night air that meant Sara could survive farther inland.

She caught up to him on the other side of the flood-plain. "I body-surfed the man to shore upriver. He's bruised but breathing." She smiled and added, "I also tipped the boat over to give the two goons some of their own medicine. Let's see how well *they* do with the crocs and—"

She noticed that the Baron wasn't listening. He stood rooted like a palm tree with his eyes fixed on the ground ahead. Sara looked down and saw a six-foot snake stretched across the path like a speed bump. The serpent had crawled out of a nearby field to soak up the warmth of the trail.

Moving only his lips, the Baron said, "It's a cobra like the one on pharaoh's crown. Only this one's alive, which I won't be if it strikes." He knew its neurotoxic venom caused respiratory collapse and painful death. The thought of being bitten had paralyzed him—except for his heart, which was busy bruising the inside of his ribcage.

Sara swished past him and directly into the cobra's line of sight. The snake arched its neck at the sudden approach and raised its puffed head three feet off the ground. Instead of retreating, the nymph stepped closer and wiggled a bare calf in the reptile's face.

Taunting a cobra is about as smart as pulling a lion's tail. With blinding speed, the serpent lunged and sank its fangs into—nothing! What looked like skin and bones was only mist and vapor. Sara backed up a few paces and offered the other leg. Once more the snake bit.

With the path now clear, the Baron bolted. He did a hundred-yard dash in ten seconds. He heard Sara's musical giggle and didn't care whether she was laughing at him or the cobra, which was spitting mad at being fooled. By the time she caught up to him, her image seemed to be fainter.

"What's the matter?" he panted, hands on knees.

"I'm drying out."

"Then you'd better get inside." He held up her tube. "Thanks for all your help. See you next time."

Sara frowned, but she knew she could go no farther. "Be careful," she whispered as she dissolved.

"Always," the Baron said. He capped the vial and started walking—until he heard noises coming from the river. Then he took off! When he reached the narrowest part of the trail, an idea popped into his brain. If he could cause a landslide, it would slow down his pursuers. He scanned the walls in the fading light for the best spot to do the most damage.

Seeing a promising groove beneath a sizable overhang of stone, he scampered uphill and cleared the loose dirt from the spot. Then he reached into the belly pack he always wore. Only when his fingers could not find the plug of C-4 did he remember using the plastic explosive at the watery entrance to the city of the Sasquatch.

The sound of footfalls in the near distance meant company was closer than expected. Aaron slid down to the path and ran. Glancing over his shoulder, he saw two hulking shapes moving in. How had they caught up so quickly?

Still a mile to the tomb, the Baron judged.

He would never make it.

Death Valley

THE Baron raced through the valley of the shadow of death. He feared the evil that was chasing him and sprinted so hard that he lost his sandals. The sharp gravel quickly made hamburger of his feet. When he could go no farther, he turned to face his pursuers. No way could he defeat the giants bearing down on him, but at least he could meet his end like a man.

The closest Nubian was thirty yards away and closing. His muscular legs churned up the steep grade. His dark face revealed neither strain nor emotion as he moved with the calm detachment of an expert killer.

Even as the Baron fumbled for his switchwhip, he knew it was too late. Just then, a smattering of stones spilled onto the path from above—followed a moment later by a boulder the size of a small car!

The rock made roadkill of the Nubian.

The Baron was paralyzed with relief. Where had that blessed boulder come from? He looked up and saw a finger of bright light on the hillside.

The Sword of Truth!

"Matterhorn!"

Matterhorn didn't have the breath to respond to his name as he zigzagged down the perilous incline. He watched helplessly as the second Nubian stepped over his fallen comrade and drew his weapon. He would be on the Baron any second!

Through the still night air came a pulsing *swoosh-swoosh-swoosh*. The Baron didn't see the boomerang that hit the Nubian in the neck, but he did see the big man clutch his throat and drop to his knees. The blow had crushed his windpipe. He fell face-first in the dirt.

By the time Matterhorn made it down the hill, Nate was picking up his boomerang and checking the Nubian's pulse.

The Baron sucked in a great gulp of relief. "How'd you know I was in trouble?" he rasped.

"You're always in trouble," Matterhorn said with a grin. "Truth is, I got an idea of how Sara could help us catch the man from Giza. Remember how she iced the pirate ship in Ireland? I figured she could do the same to his barge. So I ran back to talk to her before you got too far from the river."

"But what were you doing up on that hill?"

"I don't have your sense of direction," Matterhorn admitted. "I got lost and wound up on the path to another tomb. When I saw you being chased, I knew I couldn't climb down in time so I used my Sword as a lever and sent a rock instead." He rapped the diamond shaft against a stone and added, "The blade is unbreakable. It even multiplied my strength."

"Your aim was perfect," the Baron said.

"Nate's the one with perfect aim," Matterhorn said, nodding at the bushman. "I didn't know you were coming."

"Wouldn't have missed it, mate." He took out his knife and came toward the Baron.

"What are you doing?" Aaron asked warily.

"Bandages." Nate sliced strips from the Baron's tunic with a blade sharper than a scalpel. He used the coarse fabric to wrap Aaron's bloody feet. Then he took one arm while Matterhorn grabbed the other. Together they started toward the tomb.

After only a few steps they heard a Darth Vader breathing noise. They turned as one to see the nearest Nubian rising from the dirt. His labored breath came more easily as the bones in his throat healed. Blade in hand, he struggled to his feet and stumbled forward. He grew stronger with each step. White-hot anger burned in his dark eyes.

The Nubians were more than trained assassins. More than mere mortals. They were wraiths!

Matterhorn stepped between his friends and the oncoming dark spirit and automatically assumed fighting stance. Because his vision had adjusted to the gloom, he did not illuminate his blade.

The wraith, maddened with fury and addled by a lack of oxygen, saw only a lone figure with an ordinary sword. That's why he charged. He swung a mighty roundhouse blow that should have knocked any man halfway to the Nile. But this human stood his ground—meeting force with force. Steel and diamond clashed, sending sparks upward into the night. Both fighters danced for the advantage of higher ground.

The first time Matterhorn had crossed swords with a wraith, all he could do was hold on for dear life as the Talis protected him, moving under its own power. Now his adult body knew all his adolescent body had learned by diligently practicing kendo. He became one with his weapon, which accepted his direction and gave his blows superhuman power. He was glad he no longer wore the stolen medallion; the pain in his chest would have been unbearable.

Matterhorn flowed smoothly into *issoku itto maai*—one-sword, one-step distance—the critical spacing where a step back would thwart an attack while a step forward would allow him to strike. His feet and hands remembered what they had been trained to do, leaving his mind free to plan ahead. He recalled Kyl's words: "A warrior must know how he will end a fight before he starts one."

An idea formed as he fought and he began looking for *ken tai icchi*, the perfect opening. It came a few blows later when the Nubian's shaft slapped broadside against his and twisted. Instantly, Matterhorn slid his blade down hard into the unprotected hand.

The cut would have only wounded a man, but to a dark spirit, any contact with the Sword of Truth was fatal. Black smoke spewed from the gash instead of red blood. A sickening sulfur smell choked the air as the wraith sizzled and dissolved. His sword fell harmlessly onto the pile of smoldering clothes.

Matterhorn's grip did not loosen; his legs did not relax. The battle wasn't over. Out of the corner of his eye, he saw the wraith who had been crushed by the boulder begin to stir. These foul creatures were impossible to kill by normal means. Their bodies were disguises they wore when traveling, tools they could repair at will.

The long day of walking and rowing and running and fighting had completely drained Matterhorn. Talis or no, he didn't have the energy for more hand-to-hand combat. He wasn't even sure he could help get the Baron back to the portal. So before the second wraith could fully regain his senses, Matterhorn walked over and laid his Sword on the creature's neck.

Furlough

"Y OU handle that Sword like a master," Nate said as the trio trudged uphill in the dark.

Right now, Matterhorn was using it like a cane. "I've been studying kendo," he said wearily. "I don't go along with its spiritual teachings, but the fighting techniques have really helped me. Still, I have a lot more confidence in the Maker's Talis than my martial arts training."

That was the end of the talking until they reached the storage room in the heart of the portal tomb. The tenseness in Jewel's face eased when they arrived, but returned when she saw the gory rags on Aaron's feet. Nate went down the hall to get Kyl and Elok—who had no idea there had been trouble—while Jewel tended to the Baron's wounds.

Matterhorn dropped down next to his pack. What he wanted more than anything right now was a glass of iced tea and a long bath. He settled for a drink of lukewarm water and a wet cloth for his face. He was too tired to add anything when Kyl and Elok pressed the Baron for details about the wraiths.

"Everywhere I've gone as a Traveler, I've run into these vicious creatures," Matterhorn said.

"I am not surprised the heretics have recruited dark spirits," Elok replied. "They have no doubt been promised freedom and power on Earth in exchange for their help."

"That must be why they're willing to risk unprotected time travel," the Baron said.

"They're fallen Praetorians, right?" Jewel asked. "How many of them are there?"

"Not many," Elok said. He looked at Matterhorn and added, "Fewer now, thanks to you."

"Why don't you just execute a Praetorian when he goes bad?" the Baron asked.

"Capital punishment is not our way," Kyl said. "Exile to the island of Hesselis has been sufficient to deal with the few criminals in the Realm."

"Sounds familiar," Nate muttered. "Hesselis must be your Australia."

"What now?" the Baron asked.

Kyl leaned forward and rested his hands lightly on his knees. "In the morning we will head downriver."

"What about grabbing the man in yellow before he gets to Giza?" Matterhorn told them his idea of having Sara waylay the barge.

This confused Kyl and Elok until the Baron explained about the water nymph. When they understood, Elok shook his head. "We do not want to catch him just yet."

"Why not?" Jewel asked.

"Better to track a dingo to his den," Nate said. "Catch the whole pack that way."

"Spoken like a hunter," Elok said approvingly.

"Can we travel portal-to-portal instead of by boat?" was Jewel's next question.

"There is no reason to get there before our quarry," Kyl said. "The pyramid will be well guarded." He rubbed the skin between his bloodshot eyes and added, "It is obvious why the heretics want Giza. As a sacred crypt, the pyramid is sealed off from the outside world. It is an ideal location to hide gold and other supplies."

Kyl studied the weary but willing Travelers. The Baron's one arm and two feet were heavily bandaged. He could barely walk. Matterhorn was sunburned and exhausted. Jewel looked desperate for a good night's sleep. Only Nate seemed none the worse for wear. Having grown up in the outback, hardships were his usual lot.

"There is no need for any of you to make the trip," Kyl told them. "Use the Traveler's Cube to go home and rest. Come back in two weeks and join Elok and me downriver at Saqqara. We will go to Giza from there."

Matterhorn pulled at the hair behind his left ear and thought this over. He had been traveling for what seemed like forever. A few nights in his own bed and some home cooked meals would be wonderful. "Sounds good to me," he replied.

"I would love to see my mom," Jewel said anxiously. "If you're sure it's okay."

Kyl nodded.

The Baron patted his pack. "I'm running low on supplies." He was also thinking about how the time trip would heal his injuries. Then there was the baseball game he wanted to pitch on Saturday.

"I'll stay for the Nile cruise," Nate said. "Haven't been on safari in a while."

"This is not a hunting expedition," Elok said.

"Safari is Swahili for journey," Nate explained.

It was settled. The Baron stood up and stretched. He took out his Cube and said to Jewel, "Ladies first."

"Save that for Matterhorn," she said. "I can travel portal-to-portal."

"But it's a two-hour walk from the portal cave to your house," the Baron said.

"I don't mind. It helps me get used to being a kid again."

"I'll go along to keep you company," the Baron said as he peeled off his tattered tunic and donned his red corduroy cap.

Before leaving, Jewel pulled the guys into a group hug. "A princess couldn't ask for a better court," she said with misty eyes. "I have the bravest knight, the cleverest magician, and the sneakiest scout in the world."

"And we have the prettiest jewel," the Baron said. "But let's not get all mushy. Ready?"

"Ready." Waving to Kyl and Elok she said, "See you in a few weeks."

The Baron and Jewel stepped into the shadows and disappeared—and an instant later the Baron walked past Matterhorn into the center of the room from the opposite direction.

This presto-chango caught Matterhorn off guard. He hadn't even started to pack his gear.

"What are you waiting for?" the Baron said. He tapped his ear and added, "Don't forget your U-Tran. Do you want to keep it or shall I?"

"I'll keep it," Matterhorn said as he removed the clear throat patch and earplug and put them in their case. "How are you going to Cube me home since you don't know where I live?"

"The Sword will take you home. I'll tag along so I know where to pick you up in two weeks."

It only took Matterhorn two minutes to get ready. He exchanged a Traveler's salute with Nate and asked, "Can I bring you anything from the future?"

"I'm out of Luwak berries. You could swing by—"

Matterhorn laughed. "Sorry, I don't do droppings. How about some peanut butter cookies?"

Nate stuck a finger down his throat.

When Matterhorn saluted Kyl and Elok, the latter said, "Queen Bea would be proud of you, Wraith Slayer. And I would be proud to fight by your side anytime." Shifting his unblinking gaze to the Baron and Nate, he said, "That goes for all of you."

"The Maker protect and keep you until we meet again," Kyl solemnly intoned as the Baron and Matterhorn prepared to leave. "Serve well."

"Serve long," they replied in unison. Then in his best attempt at a German accent, the Baron declared, "We'll be back."

Epilogue

IT was getting dark when Matt plopped into the bean-bag chair in The Loft. He felt small and shriveled in his twelve-year-old body, but the trip to the present had healed his wounds and lifted his spirits.

"So this is what you look like as a kid," the Baron chuckled. "I can see the resemblance." He glanced around the tree house and gave it a thumbs-up. "Wish I had a place like this."

"Drop by anytime," Matterhorn said, staring at the thirteen-year-old Aaron.

"Pick you up in two weeks," the Baron replied. He deftly adjusted the Traveler's Cube and disappeared. Matterhorn pulled the red leather hilt from his belt and stuffed it under the beanbag. He would get it later when he could explain this addition to his growing sword collection.

There was no sign of the book through which he had been transported into the distant past. Had someone been here and taken *The Sword and the Flute*? He climbed down from the tree house and shuffled across the shaggy grass to the back door.

"Has anyone been in The Loft?" he asked his mom as he entered the kitchen.

"Just you, dearie," his mother said, taking a plate from the cabinet and piling it high with dumplings and curry. "Louise is at Macy's for the weekend."

Matt gladly accepted supper. His mom's curry was very spicy, so he also took a cup of hot tea to his room, the best thing to cool his tongue. He said hello to Reepicheep and put the rat on the bed next to him while he ate. Reepicheep sat up on his hind legs and begged for a bite. Matt nudged him away from the plate. The curry was potent enough to cook a small rodent from the inside out.

After eating, Matt went to the mirror and slowly removed his shirt. The sight of his hairless chest came as a great relief. The scar from the stolen medallion was gone, but not the memory of its lesson.

Returning to his bed, he wrote some notes in his quote book with its stubby yellow pencil. Then he turned on his computer and went hunting for Tutankhamen. He found no references to how Egyptian history should have been. No great library at Thebes. No expansive canals. No peace treaty. He shuddered at how easily the stream of history had been diverted into another course. And only four kids knew it should have been otherwise.

When he could stay awake no longer, he crawled under the covers and into a deep sleep. He dreamed of Seymour and Bertha, Kyl and Elok. He tossed and turned as he relived outtakes from his adventures.

The following day he didn't do well at the kendo tournament; he had other things on his mind.

At school on Monday, he went to the library to look for *The Sword and the Flute*. It was not on Mr. Rickets, the old bookshelf where he had first found the mysterious volume. He stopped by Miss Tull's desk to see if she had any recommendations for books on time travel.

The silver-haired librarian peered at Matt over her glasses and asked, "Science or science fiction?"

"Science, please."

Miss Tull consulted her computer and jotted down a few names. "Don't ignore science fiction in your research. Writers like Jules Verne, Gene Roddenberry, and William Gibson were ahead of their time." She handed him a slip of paper.

Matt found the books and took them home. He read all evening and fell asleep thinking about Cauchy horizons and de Sitter space-time distortions. The pattern repeated itself the next few days: school, homework, supper, reading, sleep, and dreams.

On Thursday night he took a break and put together a travel kit. He removed a pair of opera glasses from their small case and crammed it with a little harmonica, a Swiss army knife, LED flashlight, toothpaste and toothbrush, U-Tran, and various other things, including a small bottle of insanity sauce and a tube of cayenne pepper to spice up the Baron's bland cooking.

He put the case in his junk drawer without a thought that it would be discovered. His parents would never go through his stuff, and his sister didn't come into his room. She didn't like Reepicheep.

On Friday evening he read in bed until after midnight and finally fell asleep with a book across his chest. Soon the dreams came and Matt imagined the young Aaron standing nearby with an overstuffed pack hanging from each shoulder. The vision squatted and whispered, "Hey, Matterhorn. Sorry to yank you out of your comfy bed, but we gotta go."

The dream was so real that Matt could smell Aaron's breath and see the worry in the blue gray eyes under the brim of the red cap.

"Wake up," the Baron said as he shook Matt.

The warm hand on his shoulder jolted Matt awake. He sat upright and peered at the phantom by his bed.

The Baron grabbed the book before it hit the floor and put a silencing finger to his lips.

Rubbing the sleep from his eyes, Matt mumbled, "What are you doing here?"

"Ssshh," the Baron hissed. "No time to explain, just get dressed." When Matt reached for his jeans, the Baron said, "Shorts and a T-shirt would be better."

Matt fumbled into his clothes without turning on the light. "Are we going back to Egypt already?"

"Nope. Here's your gear." He slid the pack off his right shoulder.

"What's in here, rocks?" Matt said as he hoisted the rucksack.

"Air mostly," the Baron replied. "Don't forget your Sword."

Matt had brought the Sword from The Loft earlier in the week and had hidden it under his mattress. He grabbed the hilt and slapped it to the scritch pad on his belt. He took his travel kit from the drawer, ran his belt through the slits in the case, and settled it on his right hip. "What's the rush?"

The Baron stepped closer, Cube in hand. The bedroom faded to black. Matt's stomach twisted inside out as he heard the Baron say, "Jewel has been kidnapped."

THE END